M

ALL OUR TOMORROWS

Megan, a widow and translator for a German business run by handsome Hans Moerling, is proud of her three daughters, Flora, Daisy and Joy. Out of the blue, Daisy, still at university, announces her intention to marry Andy Pettifer. Unwilling to watch Daisy throw away a bright future, Megan is grateful for the support she receives from Ralph, Andy's father. Ralph, a doctor with a painful divorce behind him, is equally opposed to the marriage.

Books by Shirley Worrall
Published by The House of Ulverscroft:

A NEW FUTURE BECKONING
THE CALL OF THE ISLES
HOLD FAST THESE FAMILY TIES

SHIRLEY WORRALL

ALL OUR TOMORROWS

Complete and Unabridged

ULVERSCROFT
Leicester

First published in Great Britain

First Large Print Edition
published 2000

British Library CIP Data

Worrall, Shirley
  All our tomorrows.—Large print ed.—
Ulverscroft large print series: romance
1. Love stories
2. Large type books
I. Title
823.9′14 [F]

ISBN 0–7089–4249–0

Published by
F. A. Thorpe (Publishing)
Anstey, Leicestershire
Set by Words & Graphics Ltd.
Anstey, Leicestershire
Printed and bound in Great Britain by
T. J. International Ltd., Padstow, Cornwall

This book is printed on acid-free paper

1

'Hallelujah!' Megan Somerby switched off her computer and locked the back-up disk in its box.

'Did you say something, Mum?' Flora stuck her head round the door.

'I certainly did. I've spent weeks struggling with that confounded thing and it's finally finished. I must have translated the history of every ship, boat, and ferry ever built in Germany.'

'You can start on this next.' Grinning, Flora picked up an illustrated German booklet on porcelain. 'Is this another for the blond tornado?'

'It is,' Megan replied, her voice lightly scolding, 'although I do wish you wouldn't call him that.'

But even Megan had to admit that the description was apt.

Hans Moerling, whose highly successful publishing business kept Megan busy, had a habit of bursting into their lives like a tornado. On visits to the UK, blond, blue-eyed Hans usually found time to wine and dine Megan in style before he flew back to Germany.

'Sorry.' Flora laughed. 'Tea and biscuits to celebrate another completed masterpiece?'

'You're an angel.'

Megan pushed her computer against the wall and put manuscripts in the dresser. For the weekend, at least, they'd have a dining-room of sorts.

She went to the sitting-room where Joy, her youngest daughter, was sprawled across a bean bag. For a moment, she thought Joy was studying, but looking closer she realised the *Radio Times* held Joy's attention.

Megan shooed Spice, the lazy ginger cat, off the chair so that she could sit down. Sugar was nowhere in sight, and the thought unnerved her. Sugar was as volatile as Spice was lazy.

'Did I hear you say you'd finished?' Joy pushed the *Radio Times* aside and sat up.

'Yes, thanks to all those extra hours I put in. You can't imagine the relief. It's the most boring thing I've ever read.'

'I bet my physics books would beat it,' Joy grumbled. She brightened suddenly. 'Hey, let's go out tomorrow. It'll have to be the afternoon because I'm at the kennels in the morning.'

'Good idea.'

Flora came into the room carrying a tray. 'What's a good idea?' She kicked the door closed.

2

'Joy suggested we all go out somewhere tomorrow afternoon.'

'Count me in. It's ages since the three of us went anywhere.'

'Where shall we go?' Megan asked.

'The Shires.'

'Twycross.'

Her daughters spoke in unison and while they argued the merits of their choices, Megan smiled to herself, helped herself to a chocolate biscuit, and sat back to enjoy her cup of tea.

When Leicester opened the Shires Shopping Centre, she reckoned they must have had Flora in mind. The original shopaholic, she loved the place. Just riding the scenic lift was heaven to Flora.

Joy, at seventeen and the baby of the family, was the opposite. She had two nightmares; physics and shopping. Her idea of a treat was a day out at Twycross Zoo. The battles they'd had in the past, when they'd despaired of ever dragging her away from the penguin pool, were legendary.

It was thanks to Joy that Sugar and Spice had been given the run of the place, and that Spike, the hedgehog, had been allowed to wallow in luxurious hibernation alongside the washing machine and freezer in the back room.

'I've just survived an awful week at school,' Joy cried. 'I deserve a treat.'

'It's supposed to be Mum's treat,' Flora reminded her. 'In any case, I've been busy earning a living all week.'

Megan helped herself to the only other chocolate biscuit in the selection.

From the moment they were able, Flora and Joy had squabbled. They were utterly devoted to each other, but a stranger would never guess it. Fortunately, Daisy, the daughter born in the middle and currently in Manchester studying electronics, shared Megan's ability to let their squabbles wash over her head.

Megan wondered what Richard would think of his daughters if he could hear them now. Joy was exactly like him, but he hadn't even known she was going to be born. When Richard was taken ill, so suddenly, the possibility of pregnancy hadn't entered Megan's mind.

A month after his death, she realised what she should have known some time ago — she was pregnant.

Joy was Richard's final gift to her.

Unlike Flora and Daisy, who inherited Megan's dark colouring, Joy had long, fair hair, the same colour as Richard's. She was tall, just as he'd been, and she had those same gentle blue eyes . . .

'What are you thinking, Mum?' Flora asked curiously.

'Hmm? I was thinking about your dad, actually. I was wondering what he'd think if he could hear you now.'

'He'd say that, as the youngest, I should choose where we go,' Joy said immediately.

'He would not. He'd say that I should be responsible for my baby sister.'

Joy thumped her sister on the arm and the two of them collapsed on the floor, helpless with laughter.

'I'm going to have a bath.' Megan rolled her eyes at their antics. 'Meanwhile, feel free to practise any culinary skills you might have acquired.'

This remark caused even more laughter.

When Megan emerged from the bathroom, however, she heard the promising clatter of plates. She went into her bedroom and took her time getting dressed. She'd worked hard over the last few weeks and it was luxury to be pampered and let the girls get the evening meal.

There was no need to push herself so hard, but over the years it had become a habit. She and Richard had been young, very much in love, and broke. Paying the mortgage had been a struggle, and they hadn't had any spare money to invest for rainy days. When Richard died, the financial struggle had been a nightmare. Fortunately, she'd already set herself up as a freelance translator, but only in a very small way. Nowadays, she had plenty of work and the mortgage was paid off. Life was much easier, but Megan never forgot the lesson she'd had to learn.

She was about to leave the bedroom when she caught sight of the dress she'd bought for Saturday's party. It was hard to miss it.

'Whatever possessed me?' she asked the room.

Megan knew what had possessed her. Panic. On Saturday, she would be forty-five years old and, against her better judgement, her daughters had convinced her she should throw a party.

Also against her better judgement, she'd allowed Flora to drag her round the Shires Shopping Centre to find a suitable outfit for the occasion. Anything Megan looked at had been dismissed by Flora.

'No, you want something — bright.'

Eventually, Flora fell on the scarlet dress.

'Mum, this is made for you. Doesn't it make a statement? This says 'young and ready for anything'!'

'But I'm not young — or ready for anything.'

6

'Of course you are.' Flora thrust the dress at her. 'Go and try it on.'

Megan had learned long ago that it didn't pay to argue with Flora when she was shopping so she dutifully took the dress into the cubicle. In the subtle, if somewhat dim, lighting of the shop, it looked quite good. The cut flattered her slim figure and the dramatic scarlet added warmth to her dark colouring.

'Wow!' Flora said when Megan emerged from the cubicle. 'What did I tell you? It looks stunning, you look stunning.'

'Is it really me, though?' Megan asked doubtfully.

'It most certainly is. I'm proud of you, Mum. You don't look a day over thirty-five.'

Basking in these words of encouragement, Megan handed over a ridiculously large amount of money for the scarlet dress.

Looking at it now, she consoled herself that the party would be a small affair, just her parents, her in-laws, daughters and a few very close friends. They were kind, generous people who'd put it down to mid-life crisis . . .

When she went downstairs, the lasagne (straight from the freezer to the oven) was almost ready and the dispute had been settled.

'We're going to Twycross,' Joy announced happily.

Megan wasn't surprised to learn that Flora had given in. A talented and ambitious journalist who would stop at nothing to get her story, Flora was like dough in her sister's hands.

Perhaps it was because Flora and Daisy were so young when Richard died, and Joy arrived so soon afterwards to help fill the gap, that they both spoilt 'the baby'. Or perhaps helping Megan with Joy from such an early age had brought out their maternal instincts.

Eating off their laps while watching television was getting to be a habit — as if the absence of Daisy meant it wasn't worth setting the table. Flora took charge of the remote control and flipped from channel to channel in search of something worth watching.

They caught the tail end of the news and the weather forecast — more April showers — then pitted their wits against contestants on a game show.

They didn't hear the car stop outside. The first thing they heard was a key in the lock.

'Daisy?' Megan was in the hall before Daisy managed to close the door. 'Daisy!'

Megan hugged her daughter tight, hardly seeing the selection of bags Daisy was scattering over the carpet.

'What are you doing here? Why didn't you ring? You've got your chargecard, it doesn't cost you a penny!'

For the next few minutes, it was bedlam as greetings and hugs were exchanged.

Megan's daughters were such different individuals. Flora, with her short no-nonsense hairstyle, had to make her own voice heard. Daisy, with dark shoulder-length curls, was patient and easy-going. Joy, long fair hair tied carelessly in elasticated black velvet, was content to go with the flow.

Megan had worried herself silly when Daisy left home. She was quieter than her sisters. She wasn't shy, none of Megan's daughters knew the meaning of that word, but more reserved.

Surprisingly, though, she'd blossomed at university. From the very first moment, she'd loved it. She loved the work, she loved the social life.

'How did you get here?' Megan asked when she could get a word in.

They drifted into the sitting-room.

'A friend gave me a lift.' Daisy didn't quite meet her mother's gaze.

'But you're coming next weekend,' Flora

9

reminded her. 'You have to, it's Mum's party.'

'I'll be here,' Daisy promised. 'This visit's as well as, not instead of.'

Megan had other things on her mind, like the way Daisy was avoiding any eye contact.

'Tell me about the friend who gave you a lift.' Megan didn't miss the blush on Daisy's face.

'His name's Andy Pettifer,' she said softly. 'We met at Janice's party a couple of months ago. His brother's band did the music.'

'And he lives in Manchester?' Flora put in.

'No.' Daisy shook her head. 'He lives here. In Leicester, I mean.'

'So what was he doing in Manchester?' Flora suspected a good story.

'Visiting me,' Daisy answered, sounding defensive.

'So he's a boyfriend,' Joy said, 'as opposed to a friend who happens to be a boy?'

'Yes.'

Megan felt a twinge of alarm. Daisy was nineteen and this Andy would be a man, not a boy.

She scoffed at her own thoughts and reminded herself again that Daisy was nineteen. Of course she would have boy-friends, probably dozens of them before she got her degree.

'What's he like?' Flora asked eagerly. 'Not bad? Dishy? Drop-dead gorgeous?'

'Drop-dead gorgeous.' Daisy laughed happily. 'He's nineteen. His dad's a GP in town. He has a sister, Sarah, and two brothers, Mark and Jack. Mark's at medical school and Jack's the one in the rock band.'

'What does Andy do?' Megan asked.

'He spent a few months back-packing round Australia and New Zealand and he's hoping to get into university next year.' Daisy looked at Megan. 'I thought you could invite him to your party, Mum.'

'Yes, why not? We'd like to meet him.'

'You could ring him,' Daisy went on. 'It would be nicer if the invitation came from you.'

'OK,' Megan agreed.

'You could invite his family, perhaps,' Daisy suggested. 'I haven't met any of them yet. Mark will be away, but Sarah and Jack might like to come. So it'll be four, with his dad. Is that OK?'

'What about his mother?' Megan asked.

'His parents were divorced years ago. She married again and lives in America. Andy's dad brought them up.'

Daisy, eyes bright, went to stand by the fireplace. Megan thought she was going to say something more, but she remained silent.

'Is it serious? The real thing?' Megan tried to speak lightly.

'Yes.' Daisy opened her mouth to speak, then closed it again.

She went into the hall and came back carrying one of the bags she'd brought home. 'Washing,' she murmured, opening one of them. Like a conjuror pulling a rabbit from a hat, she produced a bottle of champagne. 'Andy splashed out and bought two bottles. One for his family and one for ours.'

'Champagne?' Joy was impressed. 'He must be loaded.'

'No, he's broke.' Daisy laughed.

'I'll get the glasses.' Flora went to the dining-room, calling as she went, 'Tell him to bring a crate for Mum's birthday.'

Thanks to Flora, the glasses were soon filled.

'What are we supposed to drink to?' Flora asked. 'Love's young dream?'

Daisy, standing by the fireplace, took a deep breath.

'We're getting married.'

Everyone fell silent. Glasses were suspended mid-air.

'You can't be serious!' Flora's voice was a whisper.

12

'When?' Joy asked.

'As soon as possible,' Daisy told her shocked audience.

Megan put her glass of champagne on the table before she spilt it. Words were trying to tumble from her lips, but she couldn't form a single sentence.

'Are you crazy?' Flora asked in amazement.

Megan saw how the question hurt.

'Daisy,' she said at last, 'for heaven's sake, talk to us. You can't waltz in here and tell us you're getting married to someone we don't know, to someone you hardly know . . . You think you're in love with this Andy? Yes?'

'I know I'm in love with him.'

'And you plan to marry him as soon as possible? When's that? When you have your degree? When you both have jobs?'

'As soon as possible. I don't know — in a month or so, I suppose.'

'What? Why? You haven't even met his family!' Megan cried. 'You know nothing of his background. He comes from a broken home and for all you know — '

'He comes from a single-parent family,' Daisy corrected her angrily. 'Just like me.'

'I was never divorced! What's his father like? Hmm? If he can get divorced at the drop of a hat, who's to say his son can't do the same?'

13

'That was a hateful thing to say!'

'I know.' Megan put her head in her hands. 'I'm sorry.'

Megan was ashamed of the cheap gibe. And her patient, easy-going daughter was furious with her. Megan tried to speak more calmly, but she was far from calm.

'I'm not trying to come the heavy-handed parent, love — '

'That's exactly what you're doing!' Tears glistened in Daisy's eyes. 'You were the same age as me when you met Dad.'

'Yes,' Megan agreed, 'but marriage? It was three years before we married.'

'We don't want to wait,' Daisy said simply.

'Nor did your dad and I, but we had to.'

'Well, we don't!' With tears in her eyes, Daisy ran from the room.

Megan watched her go. Flora and Joy were still standing there, still holding untouched glasses of champagne. They hadn't said a word — they looked too shocked.

'Well!' Flora breathed in astonishment.

'Should we go and talk to her?' Joy asked uncertainly.

'No.' Megan saw that her hands were trembling. 'Let's all calm down a little . . .'

* * *

14

Ralph Pettifer hadn't had time to close the door on the April shower when Sarah ran into the hall. Tall and red-haired, she looked exactly as her mother had at the same age.

'Dad, something awful's happened!'

'Something awful' happened most days so Ralph wasn't too concerned. He swore that if someone addressed a letter to The Mad House, Leicester, it would find him.

'And what was that?'

'This came!' She gave him an absent-minded kiss and waved a huge form in front of him. All he saw were two words: Inland Revenue.

'They do come, sweetheart, every year.'

'Yes, but — just look at it. There are pages of it.'

'I appreciate this is major catastrophe stuff, Sarah, but might I be allowed into the kitchen to make myself a coffee? I've had a long day.'

She walked into the kitchen ahead of him and filled the kettle.

'The thing is,' she began slowly, 'I've been doing a bit of totting up this afternoon.' She sat at the table, her tax return in front of her. 'I haven't had time to work things out exactly, but I seem to have earned quite a bit of money.'

Artistic, like her mother, Sarah had been

15

designing and making her own clothes for years. Then she'd designed and made a quilt for a local handicraft competition. Flushed with success when she won that, she entered the same quilt in a national competition. When she won that, too, her face and her quilt had appeared in several glossy magazines. Inquiries had arrived thick and fast, and these days, she sat in front of her computer designing quilts while two girls made them up from her instructions.

'That's supposed to be good news,' Ralph said, making coffee for them both. 'It's when you haven't made any money you need to worry.'

'Yes, I know.'

'Then it's just as well you're a very sensible young lady who takes her dad's advice and saves a percentage of her earnings to pay her income tax.' He took off his jacket. 'Are there any biscuits?'

'The tin's empty. Have a look in the cupboard.' She flicked through the pages of her tax return. 'The thing is, Dad, although I wanted to save a percentage, just like you said, well — I needed to buy the computer and the software. On top of that, I have to pay wages, and I've just had to buy a lot of expensive fabrics.'

'I see all the chocolate ones have gone.'

Ralph sat opposite her with a couple of biscuits in his hand. 'What you're saying is that you've earned a lot of money and spent it all. Am I right?'

'Almost.' Her serious expression vanished, replaced by a mischievous grin. 'I think I've spent it all — and a lot more. So if I come for a loan, Dad — '

'Oh, no! I'm right out of loans. First, it was Mark's car and so many textbooks it would have been cheaper to buy the local library. Then Andy's car and that cheap back-packing holiday which cost me a small fortune. Then Jack's guitar — I could have bought the London Symphony Orchestra —

'Plus,' he added, 'there's the small matter of a computer. The one you needed to buy. The one you needed to buy so urgently that now you can't pay your tax bill when it comes. If I remember correctly — '

'I'll pay you back!' Sarah promised on a splutter of laughter.

'Is this before they throw you in jail for non-payment of tax or after?'

Confident that Dad knowing her troubles equalled Dad solving them, she rushed round the table to stand behind him and link her arms round his neck.

'You wouldn't let them throw your only daughter in jail. Imagine what your patients

17

would think. And what about the neighbours? Think of the newspapers — local doctor's daughter hauled off in chains — '

'Who cares about the neighbours?' He held her hands and leaned his head back to look at the daughter he would lay down his life for. 'I could have your stuff thrown out and move into the best bedroom in the house. The one the master of the house might be expected to have.'

'Ha!' She kissed him, then walked over to the fridge and took out some eggs. 'I'm making your favourite. Baked Alaska. And no,' she continued with a grin, 'this isn't my way of getting round you.

'Oh, Mark was on the phone,' she went on. 'You just missed him.'

'Is he OK?'

'The same as ever. He said he's not learning anything, he's regressing. He reckons he's so confused he soon won't know an ankle from an elbow.'

Ralph sympathised. He remembered his own days as a medical student all too clearly.

Mark would come through it, though, he knew that. His son had wanted to be a doctor for as long as Ralph could remember. He wasn't intending to follow in his father's footsteps, as he wanted to be a surgeon, but he'd had no illusions that it might be easy.

'By the way, the nomad's home.' Sarah reached for a bowl.

'Andy? Where is he?'

Despite thinking that as soon as the children were off his hands he'd take off on a cruise, Ralph always experienced the same tug at the heart when one of them returned to the nest.

'He's gone to see his mates,' Sarah explained, 'but he'll be back in time to eat.'

'Is he OK?' Ralph asked.

'Er — fine.'

Her brief hesitation put him on the alert. 'Is there something I should know?'

'I don't know.' Sarah broke an egg and separated it before turning to look at him. 'He wouldn't tell me, but he did ask what time you'd be home, and he did ask what sort of mood you were likely to be in.'

Ralph groaned.

'Not another loan, surely.'

'Oh, no.' Sarah was quick to scotch that idea. 'He promised me it had nothing to do with money. I didn't think we should both mention money on the same day.'

'That's reassuring,' Ralph said wryly, not in the least reassured . . .

★ ★ ★

19

Later, as the three of them had dinner, Ralph watched Andy closely. His son looked his usual cheery self, but it was clear he had something on his mind.

It could be anything. Having left school with good grades, Andy decided he wasn't ready for university. He wanted to take a year out to see something of the world.

Travel had always fascinated Andy, probably because of the trips he'd made to America to visit his mother. He wanted to study photography with the hope of landing himself a job as a globe-trotting cameraman.

Sarah was about to make coffee when Andy told her not to bother.

'I've got something better.' He dashed out of the room and returned brandishing a bottle. 'Champagne!'

'Champagne?' Sarah had to read the label before she believed him. 'We never drink champagne.'

'Tonight, we're celebrating,' Andy announced. 'I'm getting married!'

'Very droll,' Ralph said. 'And how can an unemployed layabout afford champagne?'

'That's not fair!' Andy laughed at the description. 'What about those six weeks I worked at Taylor's? All those hours — it ought to be illegal.'

'It probably was,' Ralph muttered.

'And there's the money Mum sent us,' Andy went on, justifying the expense. 'Anyway, it's a special occasion. I'm getting married.'

'Andy,' Sarah said patiently, 'you can only do April Fools on the first of April. It's too late now.'

'I'm serious,' he insisted.

'And who's the unfortunate bride to be?' Ralph asked dryly.

'Her name's Daisy Somerby.' Andy stood at the head of the table, looking very serious indeed. 'She's nineteen and she's studying electronics in Manchester.'

'You're in love?' Ralph ventured.

'Yes.'

'You've actually asked her to marry you?' Sarah couldn't believe it.

'Yes.'

'And if she suggested you name the day — an actual day, not a vague idea for the future — you'd outrun an Olympic sprinter,' Ralph scoffed.

'I know we're young, and I know we don't have jobs yet, or money.' Andy spoke directly to his father. 'But we're getting married as soon as possible. I don't expect you to be happy about it, but I'm nineteen. I don't need permission.' He waited a moment, then lifted his glass of champagne. 'As

21

no-one can say any of the usual things, like congratulations, I'll drink to Daisy — the girl I love.'

Ralph and Sarah exchanged astonished glances.

'Andy,' Sarah began, but words failed her.

'You expect us to take this seriously?' Ralph demanded. 'You dream your way through life. You subject us to the worst practical jokes imaginable. Then, out of the blue, you expect us to take this — this nonsense seriously?'

'I'm serious,' Andy replied, and he did look very serious, 'and Daisy is serious. The way I see it, that's all that matters.'

The phone rang and Andy sighed in frustration. Ralph shared his frustration — it was impossible to talk for more than five minutes at a stretch in this house.

Sarah answered it.

'Oh, hello there . . . Yes, he's standing right here. Just a minute.' She handed the receiver to Andy. 'It's Daisy.'

Ralph tried not to listen, but it was impossible.

'It's about the same here,' he was saying. 'Yes, I know . . . I'll come over . . . Yes, I will. I'll meet you . . . Yes, OK . . . ' He listened for a moment, then laughed softly.

'That's nice, giving the poor woman a heart attack on her birthday . . . I'll leave now, OK? . . . Yes, me too.'

Andy replaced the receiver.

'I'm going to see Daisy,' he said.

'Andy — '

The expression on his son's face prevented Ralph saying what was on his mind. 'Drive carefully,' he said instead. 'I'm sure that car's not fit to be on the road — and you've got things on your mind. We'll talk tomorrow, but meanwhile, take it easy, OK?'

Andy nodded, then left without a word.

Ralph and Sarah sat at the table, quietly considering things. Sarah looked at the champagne, but it held as much appeal for her as it did for Ralph.

'I'll make some coffee, Dad.'

'Good idea.' Ralph gave her a grateful smile.

'Do you think he's serious?' he asked after a moment.

'I think he's serious about Daisy,' Sarah answered carefully. 'But marriage — no. I think you're right. If Daisy said she wanted to get married next month, he'd run for his life. Marriage means settling down, putting someone else first. All Andy wants to do is travel the world. When he's thought about it, he'll realise that marriage would put the brakes on that idea.'

She poured their coffee and sat down at the table.

'I shouldn't worry about it, Dad.'

'Yes, you're probably right.'

But Ralph did worry.

Sarah left to take some fabric swatches to a friend, Andy was with Daisy and Jack was playing at a gig. In Ralph's day, they'd had dances or functions. Now, they had gigs.

It was so rare to have the house to himself that Ralph wished he could do something useful with his time. Instead, he worried.

Andy had no idea what marriage entailed. How could he?

When Ralph and Colleen divorced, fifteen years ago, the one and only thing they agreed on was that their four children wouldn't suffer. Ralph didn't think they had.

They were happy, out-going children. They lived with Ralph, and were equally at home when they visited Colleen and her husband in California. Sarah was the only one who didn't share a closeness with her mother. He knew she found it hard to forgive her mother for leaving them.

Because he'd hidden it from them, Andy had no idea how devastated Ralph had been when Colleen told him she'd met someone else.

24

Ralph had loved her and assumed she was happy with a home and their four children. Colleen hadn't been happy, but she'd never told him. She maintained he hadn't been there to listen. Perhaps he hadn't. And perhaps, when he had been there, he'd been too wrapped up in their children to listen.

Andy didn't realise just what the divorce had done to Colleen, either. It had broken her heart to leave her children. Ralph didn't know how she'd done it. He could still remember tearful phone calls from the other side of the Atlantic. 'Tell me about the children, Ralph. Tell me what they're wearing. Anything. How's little Jack . . . ?' In the early days, Colleen visited three or four times a year, but it broke her heart every time she had to leave them. It had been a huge sacrifice, but she'd believed, as Ralph had, that they'd be better with him, living in their own home instead of adapting to a new country, a new house, and a stepfather.

Andy had no idea that Ralph's marriage had turned out to be a pipe-dream, or that he'd spent the first years of their divorce encouraging the children to write letters and make drawings to send to their mother, while all he wanted to do was beg her to come home.

Andy knew nothing of how his father had really felt. But he would, Ralph vowed. In the morning, he would know it all.

* * *

There was a light tap on Megan's bedroom door. 'It's me, Megan. May I come in?'

It was Jackie, Megan's closest friend and nearest neighbour. 'Of course.'

'I think everything's as ready as — Wow!'

'That's exactly what Flora said.' Megan pulled a face and tugged at the red dress. 'I'm forty-five years old today, Jackie. How can I be a Wow?'

Jackie laughed.

'You look terrific. Flora was right; the dress is perfect. Cheer up, it won't be that bad.'

'It won't?' Megan gave her friend a scathing glance. 'My daughter's lost her mind. I had tears and tantrums all last weekend. She was conveniently out every time I phoned in the week. Now she's only speaking in monosyllables. Added to that, I've had to invite four complete strangers to a party that I didn't want in the first place.'

'Yes, well — ' Put like that, it didn't sound very good. 'I'm sure it will be fine. What does

26

the boy's father think of it all?'

Megan thought back to the brief phone call to Doctor Pettifer. Fortunately, Andy had mentioned the party to his father so at least he was expecting an invitation.

'He seemed quite calm,' she said, 'and very polite. He insisted I didn't want strangers at my party — which of course I don't. But I can see Daisy's point. She wants us to meet Andy in a crowd.'

And the first guests were due at any moment.

Thanks to invaluable help from Jackie, Flora, Daisy and Joy, the house gleamed and there was enough food for five times as many guests. There was nothing for Megan to do — except cringe beneath a banner that stretched the length of the sitting-room, a banner with huge red lettering that read: *Happy 45th Birthday, Mum*.

If it all became too much, she supposed she could hide behind the huge arrangement of dark red roses and lace-like gypsophila that dominated the room.

The accompanying card said: *With love on your birthday, Hans*.

The arrangement was a little over the top for her sitting-room perhaps, but the gesture had made her feel wonderfully pampered.

A car pulled up and Jackie went to the

window to investigate. 'Your mum and dad,' she announced. 'Ready, Megan?'

Megan supposed she was as ready as she ever would be . . .

Andrew Pettifer was — well, a relief Megan supposed. Smartly dressed, he was tall and dark, with laughing brown eyes. He was polite and charming, and he clearly doted on Daisy.

His father, Ralph, came as a surprise to Megan, too. For no logical reason at all, she'd expected someone older, but he was about the same age as herself. He was an older version of Andy, but with a smattering of grey in thick, dark hair.

He put her at her ease immediately. Being in her own house at her own party, she shouldn't have needed putting at her ease, but she did. He gave the impression of being able to sit down to tea in a palace or a mud hut, and being equally at home in both. During their brief chat, she'd glimpsed a sense of humour, but they didn't mention Daisy and Andy's relationship.

Sarah, his only daughter, struck Megan as a lovely girl. Tall, slim, and red-haired, she had her father's ready smile.

Jack, the schoolboy son who, according to Daisy, played in a rock band, came as a relief, too. She'd expected orange hair in a ponytail, but Jack seemed a very sensible young man.

The Pettifer family seemed to fit in easily, in fact.

Ralph chatted pleasantly to the other guests, Andy was glued to Daisy's side, Sarah and Flora hit it off immediately, and Joy was currently introducing Jack to Spike, her hedgehog.

When Megan saw Ralph step out into the garden, she followed him.

It was late and dark, the light from the dining-room shedding a dim glow over the garden.

'Am I allowed out here?' he asked apologetically.

'Of course. I just came — I thought perhaps we should talk.'

'Yes.' He looked very relaxed as he threw a casual glance back at the house. 'You're worried about your daughter being involved with someone you hardly know?'

'I'm worried she's throwing away a bright future,' Megan corrected him.

'Yes, of course.' He thought for a moment. 'My son is in love with your daughter, that much is obvious. It's the first time he's been in love, and I suspect it's a first for Daisy, too. They're at the stage when they have to be together all the time, when a second apart is a second wasted, when the sky seems bluer and the sun brighter.'

'You sound cynical.'

'No, not really.' The criticism surprised him. 'It's natural enough.'

'Yes.'

'Andy is honest, trustworthy, and he'd do nothing to hurt anyone. On the other hand,' he added carefully, 'he's very impulsive. He's not ready for marriage. He has no idea what it means.'

Megan breathed a sigh of relief. He wasn't pleased with the arrangement, he wasn't angry, he wasn't accusing her daughter of seducing his son. He was being very calm and rational about it.

'Daisy's the same,' Megan said. 'She's more naive than Flora and Joy, more impressionable.'

'I gather they only met a couple of months ago,' Ralph said.

'I had no idea Daisy was even seeing anyone.'

'No.' Ralph sighed. 'I've spent the entire week trying to talk some sense into Andy, but — ' He shrugged.

'Daisy's been in Manchester. She's been out every time I've tried to talk to her. But I won't let it happen,' Megan warned him.

'Nor I,' he assured her.

The trouble was, an inner voice reminded Megan, Daisy and Andy were past the age of consent. There was little they could do about it . . .

They were about to go back inside, when the french windows opened and Daisy and Andy came outside. Daisy's hand had been in his, but Andy put an arm around her shoulders.

Daisy wouldn't meet her mother's gaze.

'We'd like to make an announcement,' Andy said quietly.

'You'll do no such thing.' Ralph's voice was soft and pleasant, but there was something in it that would have prevented Megan arguing with him.

'This is Megan's party,' Ralph reminded his son. 'You're a guest, Andy. You'd do well to remember that.'

'Fine.' Andy spoke to Megan. 'Dad's right, I'm sorry, Megan.'

He turned back to his father.

'We won't make an announcement. We'll let people know some other way. Either way, we're getting married, whether you like it or not!'

2

Megan didn't sleep much that night — the picture of the two young people firmly stating their intentions haunted her. The next morning she rose bleary-eyed and tried to revive herself with a strong cup of coffee.

Flora was still in bed, Joy had already left for the kennels, and Daisy was in the sitting-room, staring out of the window.

'All right, love?' Megan asked softly.

Daisy nodded, her gaze on the road outside.

'This is where you're supposed to ask me what I thought of Andy,' Megan pressed on, trying to break through the communication barrier. 'I thought he was lovely. I liked the family, too.'

An old blue Metro pulled up outside.

'Here's Andy.' Daisy grabbed her bag. 'We've got an appointment to see the vicar. We don't need anyone's approval, Mum.' Daisy's mouth was set in a firm line of determination. 'As Andy said, we're getting married whether you like it or not!'

After they'd gone, Megan rang Peter, the vicar. Then she decided to call Ralph

32

Pettifer, but he was out.

'I was on the phone when he left,' Sarah explained, 'and he just said he'd be back for lunch. He doesn't have a surgery, and he's not on call, so he could be anywhere. Do you have the number for his mobile?'

'No, but not to worry. It's not important, Sarah. Just tell him I rang, would you?'

Megan wished she hadn't called. She couldn't possibly think what Ralph Pettifer could do to make her feel any better.

'Mum, why didn't you wake me?'

Megan's thoughts were interrupted as Flora dashed into the room.

'I promised to meet Angie in town.' She had one arm in her jacket while the other frantically searched for the sleeve. 'I'll be late. I'll have to skip breakfast. See you later.'

Flora was at the front door when she shouted, 'Anything I can get you?'

'No, thanks, love. I'll see you later.'

Megan stood at the window and watched Flora drive away, but her mind was on Daisy.

It was difficult to accept that Daisy, her baby, was in love and on the brink of marriage.

Megan couldn't face breakfast; she needed to be doing something. They'd cleared up after the party last night, guessing they

33

wouldn't want to face it this morning, and there was little for her to do.

Just then, the phone rang.

'You don't sound as if you have a hangover,' a familiar voice said.

'Hans!' Megan laughed. 'I don't. It was a lovely party and your roses are beautiful. You shouldn't have bothered — they're far too grand for my sitting-room, but I love them. Thank you.'

'I'm glad you like them, Megan. I wanted to call yesterday, but it was late when I left my last meeting. I didn't want to intrude on your party.'

Megan loved the sound of his voice. His English was impeccable, much better than her German. There was only the merest hint of an accent.

They discussed business for a few minutes. Megan spoke of the translation she was working on, and Hans told her of another he was sending her.

'Will you be able to treat it as a priority?'

'Of course.' She smiled to herself. Once, she'd had four manuscripts to translate, each one marked 'priority'.

'I'm hoping to be in London in a week or two,' he went on, 'so don't make plans Megan.'

They had become very good friends and

Megan was looking forward to his visit already, but as soon as they'd said their goodbyes, her thoughts returned to Daisy.

Knowing there was little she could do right now, she went outside into the garden, armed with her secateurs. There were two particularly straggly shrubs threatening to take over the garden, ideal candidates on which to take out her frustration.

She had always enjoyed gardening. In fact, the large overgrown garden had been the main attraction for Megan when she and Richard decided to buy the house, all those years ago.

The two shrubs, however, soon put her enjoyment to the test. Healthy new growth caught in her hair and her clothes, and scratched her hands.

She straightened when a dark blue car stopped by the gate.

Ralph Pettifer got out.

Dressed casually in jeans and a shirt, he threw his car keys in the air and caught them as he walked towards her. He looked as if he didn't have a care in the world.

'Hello, Megan. Sarah said you rang.'

'Yes.' She pulled off her gloves and tugged at a twig that had tangled itself in her hair. 'She didn't disturb you, did she? It wasn't important.'

'No, she didn't.'

Ralph reached up and took another twig from her hair.

'Thanks.' She must look a mess. 'I rang in a moment of panic,' she admitted. 'Andy called for Daisy. They've gone to see the vicar. Did you know?'

'No!' His surprised frown turned to a look of angry impatience.

'I rang Peter, the vicar,' she went on, 'but he can't stall for long.'

'You rang the vicar?' He laughed suddenly. 'Can he stall at all? Do vicars lie?'

'This one had better,' Megan murmured. 'If he doesn't, he'll find his church full of dust and empty of flowers. And he'll be looking for someone else to do the teas at the fete.'

Ralph laughed again but all Megan could manage was a poor smile.

'Sorry. Would you like to go inside? Tea or coffee?'

'No, thanks. I've just had coffee.'

Megan ran her fingers through her hair and was relieved to find no more greenery lurking there.

'How can we stop them?' she asked.

'I don't think we can, Megan. They're not stupid. They know that, sooner or later, we'll have to accept the situation. What else can we do?'

'So that's it? We just give in to them? Do you always give in?' Megan's voice held a trace of disapproval.

'Probably more than I should,' Ralph admitted.

'I was never able to.'

'It's possibly because I'm divorced,' he said thoughtfully. 'I suppose I've tried to compensate for the lack of a mother in their lives. Then there's my work. I see parents coming to terms with all sorts of heartbreaks. Sick children. Accidents. When I get home and see four healthy children — well, nothing else seems important.'

He paused before going on. 'This marriage isn't the end of the world, Megan.'

'I know, but — '

'And at least there's going to be a wedding,' he added. 'They could have visited a registry office, grabbed a couple of witnesses off the street, and told us after the event.'

'You're right,' she said, 'of course you are, but it's so hard to sit back and watch them throw away their futures.'

'Yes, I know.' He pushed his hands in his pockets. 'But as Andy keeps reminding me, they're no longer children.

'Has Daisy talked to you about their plans? Where they're going to live, how they're going to live, that sort of thing?'

'Daisy hasn't talked to me at all.' Despair welled up inside her. 'I still can't believe it. I thought marriage was supposed to be out of fashion.'

'Apparently not.'

'And we have to just sit back and watch it happen?'

'I think so, yes. And be ready to pick up the pieces when it all ends in tears, as I feel sure it will.' Ralph watched a blackbird pecking in the border. 'I've reasoned with Andy, I've yelled at him, I've threatened him — '

'How does his mother feel about it?' Megan asked curiously.

'I haven't spoken to her. I don't think Andy has, either. No, I'm sure he hasn't. She would have been on the first plane.'

'Will she be able to talk him out of it?' Megan asked, clutching at any hope she could.

'I doubt she'll try.' Ralph quickly dashed her hopes. 'We're talking about a woman who gave up four children to be with the man she loved.'

There was no bitterness, he was stating fact, but it sounded frighteningly brutal.

'Added to that,' he went on, 'Andy's her favourite. Mark was always so practical — even as a child. Colleen left and he accepted it. He gets on well enough with

38

her, but he was into other things and the physical distance between them prevented any real closeness.

'Sarah — well, everything has to be black or white for Sarah. No matter how well you dress it up, all Sarah sees is a woman who abandoned a husband and four children. And Jack was too young to miss her much.

'Andy, despite all signs to the contrary, is the deep one. He missed her a lot when she left and they're very close.

'I'll be surprised,' he added, 'if Colleen does anything more than shower them with wedding presents and tell Daisy she's the luckiest girl alive.'

Which wouldn't help at all. It would simply win affection for Colleen and drive a deeper wedge between Megan and her daughter.

'I'll talk to Andy,' Ralph promised. 'I'll aim for his conscience and try to make him see that until he has a future, a job and prospects, he has no right to marry Daisy. I'm not optimistic, but I'll try . . . '

* * *

The toaster ejected two slices of overdone toast and Daisy sat at the table to butter them.

39

She had hoped that, having been given a week to think things over, her mum and sisters would understand and be happy for her. They didn't understand at all, however, and she was beginning to wish she'd stayed in Manchester.

As if things weren't bad enough, the family were going to lunch with the Pettifers the following day. The invitation had come from Sarah, and whilst Daisy appreciated the gesture, she was dreading it.

'Mark's coming home,' Sarah had said, 'so it'll be the perfect chance for both families to get together.'

Daisy wondered what Mark would be like. Andy had promised her she'd like him, but Daisy suspected he'd be yet another person against them getting married. From what she'd heard, he was very like his father and Daisy still didn't quite know what to make of Ralph Pettifer.

She wasn't marrying the family, she reminded herself, she was marrying Andy.

Flora came into the kitchen, looking half asleep.

'Where's Mum?'

'At Jackie's.'

'Again?' Flora grinned. 'Those two would talk both hind legs off a donkey.'

It was true; they could talk for hours, and

40

often did. Daisy could remember the day, eight years ago, when Jackie moved in to the house opposite, complete with long-suffering husband, Tom, and two young tearaway sons, Sam and Ben. Megan had carried a tray of refreshments over the road to welcome their new neighbours and brought Jackie back with her. They'd been the best of friends ever since.

'I expect my ears will soon be burning,' Daisy murmured.

'Sure to be!' Flora filled a bowl with Corn Flakes and poured on milk. 'What do you expect, Daisy? Pats on the back? Congratulations?'

'Congratulations would be welcome, yes.' Daisy spread a thick layer of marmalade on her toast, but her appetite had deserted her. This was supposed to be the happiest time of her life, but everyone was treating her as if she was a child. 'Is it really so terrible for me to want to marry Andy?'

'No.' The sound of the fridge door being opened had brought the two cats trotting into the kitchen. Before they could hope for any peace, Flora had to pour Sugar and Spice a bowl of milk. Having done that, she sat at the table and sliced a banana on top of her Corn Flakes. 'It's the way you're going about it that's so terrible.'

'What's so terrible about it?' Daisy asked in amazement.

'Perhaps selfish is a better word.'

'Selfish? Andy and I are in love and we want to get married. It's what people do. How can you say it's selfish?'

Flora munched her way through a spoonful of Corn Flakes at an irritatingly slow speed.

'Quite easily,' she said at last. 'I think it's high time you thought of someone other than yourself. You could start by thinking of Mum.

'You were two when Dad died and Joy wasn't even born. Think what that was like for Mum. She was left with two kids, another on the way, hardly any money. All she had to look forward to was an uphill struggle that she had to face alone. She had to keep going for our sakes.

'Can you remember us ever going without? I can't. I can't remember a single day when she wasn't here for us.'

'It's not my fault Dad died!'

'Grow up, Daisy.' Flora scowled at her. 'I'm just saying that Mum sacrificed a lot for us. I'm not saying we owe her, that's ridiculous, but I think she deserves better from us.'

Flora finished her Corn Flakes and poured them both coffee.

'You're met the man of your dreams, Daisy, and you're desperate to marry him. Fine. Lucky you. Now, while we all know how crazy Mum was about Dad, he's been dead for seventeen years. Don't you think she'd have enjoyed being pampered by someone else? She's very attractive, and I'm sure there would have been dozens of men willing to oblige, but she never had chance to meet anyone, did she? She was too busy taking care of us. When you think of the hours she worked, the hours she still works — and for what? Not because she enjoys it, she does it for us.

'If you'd just agree to wait, Daisy. If you'd just give Mum time to see that you and Andy are right for each other, that you've thought it all through — it could be a lovely day for her.'

The tears refused to be held back any longer. Daisy pushed her chair back and would have fled the room if Flora hadn't got to the door first.

'You can't fool me, Daisy. You *know* you're not going about this the right way. You knew Mum would be against you rushing into it, just as Andy knew his dad wouldn't be happy. And deep down, you know they're right.'

Standing at the window, watching Andy washing his car, Mark knew that if he was going to attempt to 'talk some sense' into his brother, it may as well be now. It wouldn't do any good, he was sure of that, but at least he'd be able to say he'd tried.

Andy turned at the sound of footsteps on the gravel.

'I thought it might be you.' He rubbed a shampoo-filled sponge over the paintwork. 'Well? Isn't this your cue to tell me I'm making the biggest mistake of my life?'

'Since when did you take notice of anything I said?' Mark certainly couldn't remember a time.

Andy lived for the moment, never planning further than the end of the day.

'You won't talk me out of it, Mark, so you may as well save your breath.'

'I'm not going to try. If you reckon you can afford to get married, then fine. I envy you. I wish I could.'

'You want to get married?' Andy laughed at the idea.

'If I'd found the woman I wanted to spend the rest of my life with, then yes, I'm sure it has lots of advantages. But I know it'll be a good few years before I can even begin to think about it.'

'Ah — but you haven't found the woman you want to spend the rest of your life with. If you had, you wouldn't be so keen on waiting.'

Mark lifted the wipers so Andy could wash the windscreen. He supposed Andy was right; perhaps if he'd met someone and fallen in love, he would feel differently.

The closest he came to romance was when he and Carol went to the cinema together. He and Carol got on well — they had a lot in common and they both knew what they wanted from life, but marriage was the last thing on their minds.

One day, he would qualify as a doctor, Carol would qualify as a lawyer, and then what?

'You could be right,' he said, 'but even if I wanted to, I couldn't afford to get married. I can hardly afford to keep myself, let alone anyone else. And you're planning to give up a career — '

'I'm not giving up anything,' Andy cut him off. 'I'm just taking a different course.'

'One that won't give you such a good qualification.'

'Maybe,' Andy agreed grudgingly, 'but it means I'll be in Manchester, and it means I'll get that qualification sooner. I'm still going to be a cameraman.'

'But you'd be a better one if only — '

'Mark!' Soapy water dripped onto Andy's feet. 'There's more to life than pounds and pence, you know.'

'Of course there is,' Mark agreed, 'but you're still a student. Technically, you're not even that at the moment. You can't expect Dad to keep bailing you out of trouble.'

Andy had the good grace to colour slightly.

'You wouldn't want that, surely,' Mark went on. 'I know I wouldn't. When I get married, I'll be the one who keeps my wife.'

'The poor girl will probably have died of old age by the time you get round to asking her,' Andy said with an exasperated grin. 'Or she'll have found someone else.'

'If she loved me, she'd wait.' He gave Andy a sharp glance. 'Is that what you're worried about? You think Daisy will find someone else if you don't marry her?'

'Of course not!'

'Good, because a wedding ring and a marriage certificate won't hold her if love won't.'

'You're just like Dad.' Andy sighed.

'Perhaps.' Mark didn't think that was any bad thing. 'And perhaps *you're* like Mum.'

'As least she takes life as it comes. She knows what she wants and she goes after it.'

'Does she?' Mark took a step back as Andy turned on the hose and began to rinse off the shampoo. 'Presumably she knew what she wanted when she married Dad.'

'Leave it, Mark.' He concentrated on rinsing his car, then stepped back and turned off the hose. 'Right, I'm going out so you can report your lack of success to Dad. And if anyone asks, I'm with Daisy. We're going to buy an engagement ring.'

He checked his pockets and grinned.

'I don't suppose you'd like to give your kid brother a loan?'

'Not a chance!' Mark was forced to laugh.

★ ★ ★

Flora wasn't sure whose idea it had been to come to Bradgate Park, but it had been a good one.

Sarah's lunch had been a revelation. 'As the only female living with four men, you either learn to cook or starve,' she'd said. Sarah had done the former. Not only had the food — roast beef with all the trimmings — been cooked to perfection, the presentation had been beautiful. Flora cooked the occasional meal at home, but a lot of it came from packets and the thought of catering for nine would have horrified her.

It must have been Ralph's idea to visit Bradgate Park, Flora decided. At least, he'd been the one to sort out the cars. 'I expect Andy and Daisy will want to go on their own,' he'd said dryly. 'Some of you can come with me and some with you, Mark. OK?'

Now, walking through the park, Flora could see her mum, a good way in front, laughing at something Ralph said. It was good to see her laugh — she'd done precious little of that during the last week.

Flora glanced over her shoulder. Somewhere, so far behind they were no longer in sight, were Daisy and Andy.

'I hope this isn't going to turn into one of Dad's famous hikes,' Mark said with a wry smile. 'He's a great one for walking.'

'So's Mum.' Flora looked at her heels in dismay and he laughed.

'Don't worry. Sarah firmly believes that if God had expected us to walk, He wouldn't have let us invent cars.'

Flora wondered what it was about the Pettifer family that made them so easy to be with.

Sarah had described Mark as 'great — nothing to look at and a bit serious at times, but a great brother'.

Nothing to look at?

He was as tall as Andy, but broader across the shoulders. His hair was a fascinating mix; thick and dark like his father's, but with a hint of Sarah's red. Green eyes, she'd noticed, and beautiful long, dark lashes. Nothing to look at indeed! Flora could picture him strolling along hospital corridors in a white coat — it was enough to make a girl take up nursing . . .

'Have we lost Andy and Daisy?' He looked over his shoulder.

'I expect they're busy making plans.'

'Plans?' Mark smiled at that. 'Andy's never made a plan in his life.'

'Then perhaps Daisy's avoiding me,' she said quietly. 'I gave her what I thought were a few home truths yesterday. Perhaps I was a bit hard on her.'

'Let me guess. You told her she was making the biggest mistake of her life?'

'No, it was worse than that. I told her she was being selfish.' She sighed. 'I keep thinking I ought to apologise, but it's how I feel. It's all so rushed, it doesn't feel like a proper wedding.'

'I know. I had a phone call from Dad

telling me I had to talk some sense into Andy, quickly followed by a call from Andy asking me to be his best man! I still can't quite believe what's happening.'

'Awful, isn't it? And I *do* think she's making the biggest mistake of her life. Not because of Andy, I like him and I think they're well suited, but they hardly know each other, and Daisy's so — oh, immature, I suppose.

'I tried talking to Andy,' Mark said, 'but I chose a bad time. He was going to meet Daisy and buy an engagement ring. Is she wearing one?'

'No.' It was the first Flora had heard about it. 'You don't think — no. I was wondering if they'd had second thoughts, but it's clear they haven't.' She paused briefly. 'What does your mum think about all this?'

'I don't think she knows yet.'

'Sarah said you got on well with your mother,' she ventured.

'Yes, I do. Not that I see her very often. I haven't been out to California for over a year. It's OK, but it's not home.'

'OK?'

'It's not all it's cracked up to be.' Mark laughed at the doubtful expression on her face. 'Everyone thinks of LA, Hollywood,

San Francisco and Clint Eastwood walking round every corner, but Mum lives near Sacramento and it's not very glamorous. We've done the Beverly Hills and Bel Air tours, but the houses are well hidden and no-one walks the streets so you don't see anyone of interest. The weather's good, of course, but you soon get tired of sunshine.'

'You do?'

'I do.' He laughed at her disbelieving expression. 'I'm always glad to get home. Of course, that's probably more to do with staying with Mum and Tony than the sunshine.'

She frowned, puzzled.

'As much as I adore them both, I find it a bit trying. Tony must spend the whole year planning the most complicated trips for us, and I always feel we should be terribly grateful when, really, we'd much rather do something else. Yes, we're quite close, but Mum's life is there with Tony, and ours is here.'

★ ★ ★

The following day, Ralph sat behind his desk and wondered what they'd done to deserve such a chaotic morning. Thankfully, the last patient had gone and he thought he

51

might — just might — manage lunch.

Penny, his partner, knocked on his door, checked he was alone and closed the door after her.

'Can I hide in here?' She threw herself down in the chair opposite him, yawned, and ran her fingers through her short, blonde hair. 'What a morning!'

'Awful. But it's over. Do you have time for lunch?'

'Not a hope. Dinner tonight?'

'We can try, but I'm on call,' he warned.

'Who'd want to be a doctor?' A quick smile lit her face. 'Mark would. How is he? Did you have a good weekend?'

'Mark's fine. Struggling with the work, but that's not new. And yes, thanks, it was a very good weekend. After lunch yesterday, we all went to Bradgate Park. It's amazing the way both families get on so well.' He smiled wryly. 'It's just a pity Andy and Daisy get on so well.'

'They're nineteen, Ralph.'

'Nineteen going on nine.'

'Stop worrying, it will all work out for the best.'

'That's easy for you to say.'

Penny had no children. Forty-four years old and divorced for five years, she seemed happy enough living alone, but Ralph couldn't help thinking it was a waste. She was a warm, fun-loving person. Attractive, too.

'Where shall we go for dinner?' he asked. 'As you're on call, we'd better go somewhere we don't have to book. Do you fancy Chinese for a change?'

'Sounds good to me.'

Just then, Val's voice crackled on the intercom.

'Ralph, it's Colleen.'

'OK. Thanks.' Ralph looked at his watch, did a mental calculation, then frowned at Penny. 'It must be around three in the morning over there. OK, Val, I'll take the call.'

'I didn't mean she was on the phone, Ralph,' Val said, a little apologetically. 'She's here — as in on the premises.'

'*Here*? In the building?'

'That's right.'

Penny smiled at the astonished expression on Ralph's face.

'Bang goes dinner.'

'It looks like it. Penny, I'm sorry.'

'Don't be. The way today's going, it would have been a disaster anyway.' She stood up, leaned across his desk and brushed her lips against his cheek. 'Tomorrow can only be better.'

53

'Why do they sound like famous last words?'

Laughing, she opened the door.

'I'll catch you later.'

Ralph tried to gather his thoughts. At least Colleen's presence explained why Andy hadn't been able to reach her over the weekend. Ralph had been secretly pleased. Perhaps he was being unfair, but he couldn't imagine Colleen doing anything to help the situation.

But what was she doing here?

He left his office and walked into the reception to find out. Colleen had been flicking through an old copy of Good Housekeeping, but she jumped up and crossed the room to him.

Every time Ralph saw her, he was taken aback by how beautiful she was. A strict diet and lots of exercise kept her as slim as ever, and her dark red hair had been expertly cut so that only those closest to her would know how unruly those thick curls were. Looking at her, he couldn't help remembering the speed with which he fell in love with her, and the way no-one born could have persuaded him to wait until he qualified before he married her.

'Ralph!' She threw her arms round him, kissed him, then drew back to look at him.

'Tony had to fly to London for a few days so I decided to come with him and surprise you all. I've been to the house, but there's no-one there.' She laughed, green eyes shining with excitement. 'Surprised?'

3

This surprise visit was typical of Colleen, Ralph thought, as he drove home from the surgery. Colleen was following in her green hired car.

It would never have dawned on her to plan ahead and make a simple phone call. It was obvious where Andy's impulsive nature came from!

He pulled into his driveway, parking close to the garage so that Colleen could park behind him but, perversely, she parked alongside, blocking Sarah's car and making it almost impossible for him to open his door and get out.

'I need my cases,' she told Ralph as she got out of the car.

Cases? It hadn't crossed his mind that she might be staying, but it was obvious she would. She could hardly drive from London, stop for a bite of lunch, and return.

'How long are you planning to stay?'

'Only two nights, I'm afraid.'

He dragged her cases from the boot and smiled to himself.

'I see you've brought the kitchen sink.'

She laughed.

'You know how it is, Ralph.'

He did. He'd been on holiday with Sarah enough times to know. It was a standing joke in the family that the distribution of suitcases was one for Sarah, and one for the rest of them.

As he carried the cases in to the hall he heard an upstairs doors closing, followed by the sound of light footsteps.

'Dad? What are you doing — ' Sarah turned the corner and stopped. 'Mum?'

'Sarah!'

Sarah only just managed to get to the bottom of the stairs before Colleen rushed forward and hugged her tight. Sarah's horrified expression, as she looked at Ralph over Colleen's shoulder, was an echo of his own feelings. He shook his head slightly which she could take to indicate that he was as surprised as she was, or that he hadn't mentioned Andy's wedding plans.

'Mum, what are you doing here?'

'Just a flying visit, darling. I wanted to surprise you all.' Colleen held Sarah away from her. 'Just look at you.' Beaming, she turned to Ralph. 'Isn't she beautiful, Ralph? We did a good job, didn't we?'

'We?' Sarah's voice held a trace of resentment that Ralph knew well. It was lost on Colleen, however.

'She takes after her mother,' he said truthfully.

'Only in looks.' Sarah moved to her father's side.

It was uncanny how alike they were. Even the colours they wore were the same. Colleen's tailored black trousers were teamed with a green silk shirt. Sarah was wearing black jeans and a green T-shirt. Colleen's shirt was fastened at the throat by a gold clasp and Sarah wore a gold chain around her neck.

The similarities were easy to spot but the differences were more subtle. Sarah's expression was difficult to define. The spark of resentment in her eyes gave her an almost childlike appearance. Ralph knew that part of her longed to love her mother, but another small part of her refused to.

Colleen's thoughts were difficult to guess. The glowing smile and the carefully applied make-up didn't quite conceal the weariness in her eyes. Ralph had the sudden feeling that all was not right in her world, and it surprised him.

'So where is everyone?' Colleen asked.

'We are everyone,' Sarah replied dryly. 'Mark's in London, Jack's at school and Andy — ' her hesitation was only brief ' — Andy's in

Manchester, visiting a friend.'

They were equally reluctant to tell her of Andy's plans. Ralph liked to think it was a noble gesture, leaving Andy the chance to impart the good news himself, but he knew, deep down, that they doubted Colleen's ability to do more than push the young couple towards the aisle with ideas for flowers, dresses, invitations, receptions, and honeymoons.

'Coffee? Lunch?' Sarah suggested lamely, heading for the kitchen.

Colleen was ahead of her and was soon diving into cupboards and making suggestions. Neither seemed to have noticed that the table was hidden by a mountain of Sarah's scraps of fabric.

'It'll have to be quiche and salad,' Sarah said firmly. 'We'll have a proper meal later.'

Sarah's determination to keep Colleen out of the cupboards succeeded, and perhaps only Ralph heard the resentment beneath the veil of politeness.

'I'll take your cases up,' he said, hoping Colleen would follow him.

'Mark's room,' Sarah said. 'I haven't made the bed up yet,' she added for Colleen's benefit, 'because he only left last night.'

'I'll find everything,' Colleen assured her, turning to follow Ralph.

59

Ralph took her suitcases to Mark's room and left Colleen to make up the bed and unpack.

When he returned to the kitchen, Sarah was chopping tomatoes — viciously.

'Sarah —'

'I know,' she cut him off, 'she loves us all very much.'

'She does. She didn't walk out and leave us a note, you know. I might not have thought so at the time, but a divorce was inevitable. We discussed it all in great depth, Sarah. We both decided it would be better if you stayed here, with me. And we both decided I could cope.'

'Which you did, very well.' Her expression softened. 'But you've missed out, Dad. While Mum's been enjoying life, you've been coping with us. You should have remarried. If it hadn't been for us, you would have.'

'No, Sarah, I wouldn't.'

Contrary to Sarah's belief, marriage was the last thing Ralph had longed for over the years. The thought of her past matchmaking attempts made him smile, though. Since Penny's divorce came through, five years ago, those attempts hadn't been very subtle, either. She was convinced that he and Penny were made for each other. They were good

60

friends, very good friends, and being doctors in the same practice meant they saw a lot of each other, but neither of them was interested in marriage.

'It's supposed to be parents who nag their children to marry, not the other way round,' he said, and she laughed.

'In this family we do things differently.' She sighed. 'Take no notice of me. I'd be more pleased to see Mum if I didn't know for a fact that she'll have Andy married in no time, then fly back to the sunshine leaving us to deal with the aftermath.'

That was exactly how Ralph felt.

'But,' Sarah added, lashing out at a tomato, 'I will not have her interfering in my kitchen!'

'Hell hath no fury like a woman having her kitchen interfered with.'

Sarah was smiling. 'Do we tell her about Andy? Or do we wait until Andy turns up, which could be any time?'

'I suppose we tell her.' But Ralph wasn't enthusiastic.

During lunch, they managed to avoid all talk of Andy.

Sarah's work was discussed and Ralph was pleased to see his daughter's resentment slowly melt away. Whether Sarah liked it or not, she was exactly like her mother — and

61

not just in appearance. They both had an instinct for colour and style, and they shared the same quick wit.

Then, the subject turned to Jack. The way things looked, he would be either a rock guitarist or a vicar!

Mark's progress at medical school came next, and Colleen made several comparisons with Ralph's student days. Practically every sentence started with 'Ralph, do you remember?'

He remembered it all — so clearly it might have been yesterday . . .

Colleen had been studying history at university with no idea what she might do afterwards. She'd been a beautiful, impulsive creature — she still was — and for Ralph, it had been love at first sight. He had loved her with all his being. Everything he'd done had been done for Colleen, and for their future.

Their parents had begged them not to rush into marriage, to wait until Ralph qualified, but they had been deaf to all reason. They'd had their lives mapped out; they would marry, have beautiful children, and embrace old age as much in love as when they exchanged their vows.

Their wedding had been a lavish affair. They'd wanted everyone they had ever known to share their happiness. Confetti had rained down on them like blessings. They honeymooned in Greece, but it could have been anywhere. The sights were lost on them; they were too much in love to care. They'd laughed like children when yet another piece of confetti was discovered in an unlikely place.

Mark was born less than a year later, a perfect miracle to seal their love. Both of them had shed tears at his perfection —

'Sorry?' Ralph came back to the present with a jolt.

'Andy's visiting a friend in Manchester you say?' Colleen repeated. 'Girlfriend or boyfriend?'

'Girlfriend,' Ralph answered uncomfortably.

'What's she like?' Intrigued, Colleen directed this question at Sarah.

'Her name's Daisy and she's at university there, studying electronics. She's the same age as Andy. She lives locally and they met at a party where Jack was playing.'

'Is it serious?'

Sarah threw a helpless glance in Ralph's direction.

'Yes,' he said slowly. 'Actually, Andy spent the weekend trying to phone you, Colleen. I'm sure he'd rather tell you himself, but as he's not here — '

'Yes?' she prompted.

'They're getting married.'

* * *

It was beginning to rain when Mark reached Carol's flat. He pressed the button and hoped that, for once, one of them would hear the bell. Usually, they were making so much noise they didn't hear it.

Seconds later, Carol opened the door. Paying no heed to the rain, she threw her arms round his neck and kissed him.

'I've missed you,' she murmured.

'I've missed you, too.'

She looked a little tired, he thought, but that didn't surprise him. Becoming a solicitor was on a par with becoming a doctor; life became a merry-go-round of studying, sleeping and more studying. Perhaps Carol had done too much studying and not enough sleeping.

'We've got the flat to ourselves,' she told him as they walked into the sitting-room.

There was a delicious smell coming from the small kitchen area.

'Gemma's out with her new boyfriend,' she explained, 'and Amy and Sue have joined a keep-fit group. I thought we'd economise and eat in. There's a good film on later.'

Mark had expected to go to their usual restaurant, but the idea of having Carol to himself was far more appealing.

While she worked in the tiny kitchen space, Mark told her about his weekend; his unproductive chat with Andy, his views on Daisy, and the afternoon at Bradgate Park.

'How was your weekend?' he asked.

'Gran paid me one of her surprise visits.' She grinned. 'She dragged me away from my books, took me out for a cholesterol-laden tea, and asked me if that nice young man was still courting me.'

Mark laughed. At his one and only meeting with Carol's grandmother, he'd soon realised that the woman thought Carol's intention to be a solicitor was something she would 'grow out of' and that she should settle down with 'a nice young man'. It also became evident that she considered Mark eminently suitable.

It was from her grandmother that Carol had inherited the bubbly, fun-loving nature that had attracted Mark in the first place. She rarely failed to see the funny side of things and often regaled him with anecdotes of gaffes she or another person on her course had made, or the hilarious antics of her flatmates.

'What smells so good?' he asked.

65

'Well, if it's not me, it's beef cooking slowly in red wine. Amy donated the half bottle of wine,' Carol told him with a chuckle. 'She said it was only fit for cooking.'

Much to Mark's surprise, the table, which was usually piled high with books or make-up or both, was covered by a red tablecloth. Two red candles were lit before Carol put the food on the table.

The beef was delicious, reminding Mark that he'd had to skip lunch and was ravenous.

'Will you dash back to Leicester now that your mother's home?' Carol asked suddenly.

'No. She's having dinner tonight with Dad and Daisy's mum. Apparently Megan's German boyfriend is going to be there, too. Mum's coming back to London on Wednesday so I'll see her then.' He speared another piece of succulent beef. 'Why not come with me? You'd like her.'

'I'd like to, but — ' She looked doubtful. 'She hasn't seen you for a while and I'm sure she'd rather have time alone with you. Besides, I'd hate to give her the same ideas as Gran. Andy's given her enough to worry about, without thinking you're about to jeopardise your career as well.'

'Mum's not the type to put two and two together and make five,' Mark promised with

66

a laugh. 'She'd like to meet you. I'll arrange something with her.'

Tony would make the customary grand gesture, Mark guessed. There would be tickets to a show or something similar, along with a meal at an expensive restaurant. It wasn't that Tony tried to impress particularly, it was more a case of trying hard — too hard sometimes — to make sure everyone had a good time. Mark was never sure if he did it for them, or for Colleen.

'We'll leave the washing-up till later,' Carol broke into his thoughts. 'The film will be starting in a minute.'

'What is it?' he asked, and she grinned, a little ruefully.

'*Casablanca.*'

'It can't be.' He groaned. 'It was only on a couple of months ago.'

'Almost a year ago.' She moved two piles of clothes from the sofa, switched on the television, sat down and patted the seat beside her. 'You don't mind, do you? It's my favourite.'

'Wake me up at the end,' he told her with a grin. 'When Bogie's telling her she can't stay with him because she'll live to regret it. Just before he says 'Maybe not today, maybe not tomorrow, but soon . . . ' '

Laughing at his poor Bogart impression, she made sure the box of tissues was within reach, then sat with her feet on his lap to enjoy the film.

As the film began, Mark was trying to remember when *Casablanca* had last been shown on TV. He and Carol had watched it together, soon after they met. She was right, he realised. The months had flown so quickly and it shocked him to realise they'd been together for almost a year. No wonder her grandmother was beginning to imagine the sound of wedding bells . . .

★ ★ ★

Megan picked up the phone, tapped out the number and waited for her friend to answer.

'Tom?' His voice took her by surprise. 'What are you doing at home? Is Jackie OK?'

'Yes, she's fine.' He sounded amused. 'I've taken a couple of days off work to help a friend move his narrow boat.'

'That's nice.' Megan grinned. 'Jackie will enjoy that. She often says that the two of you don't do things together.'

'Don't you start!' Tom's deep laughter rumbled down the line. 'And don't come running to me when you can't pay your phone bill. Can't you open the window and shout?'

Jackie took the phone from him.

'I wouldn't mind him going off on these jaunts,' she told Megan, 'if I didn't have to give him enough food to keep an army on the march. So what's new?'

'I need some advice on what to wear. Colleen, Ralph's ex-wife, has turned up and I'm having lunch with them both in about three hours.'

'But I thought Hans was visiting.'

'Yes, he is. He's coming, too.'

'What's brought Colleen here? No, don't tell me. Give me twenty minutes to get Tom out of the way and I'll come over . . . '

Before Tom's car had reached the end of the road, Jackie was walking into Megan's kitchen, dressed somewhat optimistically for summer in a bright red T-shirt.

'Why is Colleen here? Has she rushed over to try and change their minds?'

'No. We'll have coffee in the garden, shall we? No, it was just a coincidence. Tony, her husband, is in London for a few days with his work and she decided to come with him.'

'So she didn't know about the wedding?'

'Not until Ralph told her. Andy's travelling

69

back from Manchester this evening apparently.'

They moved around Megan's kitchen with the ease of long friendship; Megan made the coffee and Jackie put cups and biscuits on the tray.

'Is it warm enough to sit out?' Jackie asked doubtfully.

It was — just.

Megan turned the chairs around so they faced the sun, then moved them forward, out of the shade.

'Why are you worrying about what to wear?' Jackie asked, as soon as they were comfortable. 'Is this just to impress Hans or — ?'

'No!' Megan scoffed.

'Good.' Her friend grinned. 'Because Hans would fancy you if you wore used bin bags.'

'Jackie!'

'I know.' Laughing, Jackie put up her hands in a defensive gesture. 'Your relationship with Hans is purely professional. His business keeps you solvent. I just wish Tom and I had one of those professional relationships. That way, perhaps I'd be given the most enormous arrangement of red roses I've ever seen.'

'It's Colleen I'm worried about, not Hans.' Megan scowled at her. 'I expect she'll be very

70

glamorous and I'll feel like an ageing country yokel. I've been on two planes in my life and she crosses the Atlantic on a whim. Ralph said she'd probably shower Andy and Daisy with wedding presents and tell Daisy she's the luckiest girl alive. Added to that, I gather Andy's her favourite and she'll probably consider Daisy beneath him.'

Jackie spluttered with laughter.

'What nonsense. You're not so bad yourself, Megan. Hans is certainly managing to find plenty of business in the UK. And if you had a husband in a well-paid job, and if you didn't have three daughters, you could cross the Atlantic on a whim. Not that it matters. And if she's got any sense at all, she'll see that Andy's the lucky one!'

Megan smiled at her friend's loyalty.

'And I'm quite sure,' Jackie went on, 'that she does have sense. Ralph Pettifer wouldn't have married her otherwise.'

Jackie sipped her coffee, before saying thoughtfully, 'I wonder what her husband's like. Can you imagine giving up everything — a marriage and four children — to move to a strange country?'

'No.' Megan had tried, but she couldn't.

'Can you imagine giving up a man like Ralph Pettifer?' Jackie shook her head at such insanity, then grinned. 'Apart from the fact that he's such a nice man, he's — well, I suppose he's what they mean by tall, dark and handsome. He's certainly pleasing on the eye.'

'So are his sons, more's the pity,' Megan retorted dryly. She flicked her fingers at a persistent fly. 'Did I tell you about Flora?'

'What about Flora?'

'On Sunday, when we went to Bradgate, she and Mark were walking together. There's nothing strange in that, I know. Daisy and Andy were together, of course, and Joy was discussing the horrors of physics and school in general with Jack. Age goes with age, I suppose, so Mark and Flora sort of paired off. Ralph even joked about it. He said we could arrange a triple wedding and save ourselves a lot of hassle.'

Jackie laughed and waited for more.

'So?'

'So, yesterday morning, when I said something about Mark, Flora turned the colour of your T-shirt.'

'No!' Jackie's surprise turned to amusement. 'Oh, I don't think you have any worries there, Megan.'

'No,' she agreed, 'but I haven't seen Flora blush since she was twelve.'

Flora had interviewed many celebrities,

and it took a lot to impress her. Looks alone wouldn't do it.

'Does Mark have a girlfriend?' Jackie asked.

'Yes. In London. I think her name's Carol.'

'There you are then.'

Jackie returned her empty cup to the tray and leaned back in her seat, eyes closed against the sun . . .

* * *

Megan had left the front door open so that she would hear Hans arrive. When she did, she ran down the stairs. He was in the hall, and her feet didn't have chance to touch the bottom step before his hands circled her waist and he swung her down to his level.

'Megan, you look more lovely every time I see you!' He kissed her on both cheeks.

'Megan's hands went to his shoulders for support.

'You look very smart yourself, Hans.'

A dark suit emphasised his blond good looks and highlighted his brilliant blue eyes, and, as usual, Megan was surprised to realise just how happy she was to be with him again.

They left early, giving themselves time for a drink and an opportunity to catch up on each other's news before Ralph and Colleen arrived. As soon as they drove into the hotel's car park, however, Ralph's car pulled up alongside.

While introductions were made, Megan decided that Colleen was exactly how she had pictured her. With her amazingly slim, elegant figure, the expensive-looking curve-hugging green dress, and the gleaming red hair, Colleen was an older, more sophisticated version of Sarah.

'It's wonderful to meet you, Megan,' she said warmly. 'Ralph's told me all about you.'

On Jackie's advice, Megan was wearing a blue dress she'd bought on impulse and hadn't yet worn. She'd thought it might be too dressy for lunch, but now, she was pleased she'd listened to Jackie. At least she didn't feel frumpy alongside Colleen.

As they walked into the hotel, Colleen chatted about how the landscape had changed since she lived there and how surprised she was to find the sun shining.

'Technically, I'm on call,' Ralph warned them apologetically, 'but I've had a word with a colleague and she should be able to cover for me. It's a bit tricky at the moment, as everyone seems eager for a holiday, but I think we'll be safe.'

Over drinks, Megan marvelled again at how alike Colleen and Sarah were. They had the same dignified, self-assured manner and the same sense of humour.

Colleen adopted the role of hostess and, although she did most of the talking, she was very skilled at including everyone.

She complimented Hans' faultless English, told them of her visit to Germany with her husband, Tony, then listened attentively to Megan's story of her own trips to Germany, taken many years ago.

From the way she talked about Tony, it was clear that she was very proud of the way he had turned his advertising agency into one of the most respected in America.

With their drinks finished, they were ushered to a discreet table for four and only when they had ordered did Colleen mention wedding plans.

'Ralph tells me how lovely Daisy is,' she said with amusement, 'and how well suited they are, and how much in love they are. Then he says he's determined to put a stop to it!'

'I agree with him,' Megan replied. 'They are in love, that's plain to see. They're well suited, too, but they're both so young and,

I think, a little naive. They don't seem to have a clue what marriage involves.'

'A pair of dreamers,' Ralph said with a fond smile.

Their food was brought to the table and the subject was dropped for a few minutes.

'I'll have to reserve judgement until I see Andy,' Colleen said at last, 'but if Daisy makes him happy, and it sounds as if she does, then they'll have my blessing.'

'Of course she makes him happy,' Ralph said, 'but that doesn't mean it has to be marriage.'

'You'd rather they just moved in together?'

'Yes, I would.'

Ralph's answer surprised Colleen, as it did Megan. Megan hadn't thought about it before, but now she wasn't sure how she'd feel. She supposed she'd be disappointed, but at least, living together, Andy and Daisy would be given a chance to see if marriage was really what they wanted.

'In this case, I think I would, too,' she agreed.

'Good heavens.' Colleen laughed softly. 'And I'd been thinking you were both being a little old-fashioned.'

'It's not a case of being old-fashioned or otherwise.' Ralph's voice held a trace of impatience as he spoke Megan's thoughts for her. 'It's a case of knowing your children, and knowing what's right for them.'

They fell silent.

Ralph was right, Megan thought; they were only against this marriage because they knew, without doubt, that neither Andy nor Daisy were ready to commit themselves for life. Megan and Ralph knew their children well.

Colleen was Andy's mother but did she really know him? How could she? Seeing children a couple of times a year, in something that must resemble a holiday atmosphere, simply wasn't enough.

Colleen declined a sweet but Megan, refusing to worry about calories, joined Ralph and Hans in ordering the lemon cheesecake. It was delicious and she savoured every mouthful. Treats like this were too rare not to be enjoyed to the full.

'Have you forgotten how it feels to be in love, Ralph?' Colleen asked softly.

There was something in his eyes that brought goose bumps to Megan's flesh.

'No, I haven't forgotten.'

'Then you should realise that you won't change their minds,' she told him. 'Andy's only doing what you did. Think how many people tried to talk us out of marriage, or tried to persuade us to at least wait until you'd qualified.'

'Perhaps they should have tried harder,' Ralph said quietly.

'How can you say that?'

'Easily.'

Megan shifted uncomfortably in her seat. She glanced at Hans and saw a reassuring smile in his eyes.

'You can't say our marriage was a mistake, Ralph,' Colleen insisted. 'We have four lovely children.'

'I'm unlikely to forget that, Colleen. But bringing up four children alone, with your marriage in tatters, is not the life I'd choose for Andy. Or for Daisy.' Putting an end to the conversation, he looked at Megan. 'Coffee? Coffee, Hans?'

They both accepted, but Megan wanted to leave. She liked Ralph, and much to her surprise, she liked Colleen, too, but she could almost feel the emotion sparking between them. The last thing she wanted was to get drawn into it.

She couldn't imagine how Ralph must feel. He'd loved Colleen once, and Megan had gained the impression that he'd still loved her when they divorced. There was nothing to say he didn't love her now. It must be hard for him, having Colleen remind him of happier days when, all the while, the man she'd taken for her second husband was in

London, waiting for her.

Fortunately, thanks to Hans and Ralph, conversation became easier and, once again, laughter rippled round the table.

'I'll see you again, Megan,' Colleen said as they were parting company. 'I don't know when, but I'll be back in plenty of time for the wedding.'

'It's been lovely to meet you,' Megan replied, and she was surprised to discover how much she meant it.

Hans started the car, then waited for Ralph to drive out of the car park.

'I'm sorry about that, Hans,' Megan said quietly. 'It all got a bit personal.'

'It was unlikely to be anything else,' he replied. 'Ralph and Colleen are in a difficult situation. They can't discuss their son's marriage, and his future, without remembering their own mistakes.'

'I suppose you're right. But I'm still sorry you had to witness it. It's bad enough involving you in my problems, without subjecting you to theirs as well.'

'My dear Megan.' He switched off the engine, unfastened his seat belt, and turned to face her. 'Has it never occurred to you that I might *want* to be involved in your problems?'

He touched her face with a gentleness that

was completely out of character.

Her heart was beating fast as his face came closer to hers. Instinctively, she reached towards him. His lips were cool against hers, his kiss gentle but insistent . . .

* * *

Almost as soon as they reached home, Ralph had been called out to an emergency. Colleen made herself comfortable with a book on the sofa. But her mind was elsewhere.

She was thinking about Ralph. He thought Andy was her favourite, Colleen knew that, but he was wrong. She had no favourites. Her children were all special in their own individual ways.

Mark, as her first child and the image of his father, would always have a special place in her heart. Jack, the baby of the family, with a personality that alternated between strongly independent and surprisingly loving, was equally special.

Perhaps Andy was the child she understood the most, however. They had never really lost touch over the years.

But it was Sarah that Colleen missed the most. The two of them should have shared so much. They should have been great friends and confidantes.

'Good book?' Sarah asked as she came into the room.

'Not particularly.'

Smiling, Sarah sat opposite Colleen. 'Has Tony taken up scuba-diving?' she asked suddenly and Colleen laughed.

'What do you think?'

For the last ten years, Tony had been threatening to take up scuba-diving and promising to take the children as soon as he'd learnt the basics.

Here, in the house that had once been her home, sitting quietly with her daughter, it was easy to laugh, and just as easy to forget how moody and irritable he'd been for the last few months, and how Colleen had known that, for the first time, Tony hadn't wanted her company on this trip.

Tomorrow, she would have to return to London. She would have to face again the problems in their marriage, problems that she couldn't even begin to understand.

But that was tomorrow.

'If Daisy's anything like her mother,' she remarked, turning her mind to more cheerful matters, 'Andy's very lucky. Megan's nice, isn't she?'

'She's a lovely woman.' The reply was a little abrupt, or perhaps Colleen imagined it.

'She's very lucky, having such a good relationship with her daughters.'

'I don't think luck has anything to do with it!' Sarah got to her feet, and strode back to her spot by the window. Her back was rigid with tension.

'Well, no, of course not, but you know — '

'I know Megan didn't walk out on her daughters,' Sarah snapped.

'Sarah, love, I never — '

'Megan's put her own life on hold,' Sarah cut her off. 'Just as Dad has. Have you any idea what it's been like for him? Things are easy now, but can you imagine what it was like for him, holding down a demanding job, making sure he or someone else collected us from different schools, making time for us, listening to us? Do you even care?'

'Of course I care.'

'Do you? You might pretend to care — for a few weeks of the year. You take us on trips, shower us with presents like the perfect mother, then send us on a plane back to Dad so that you can get on with enjoying your life. You don't care. Why should you?'

'Sarah!' Colleen's voice was a shocked whisper.

'Oh, Dad's told me how hard it was for you to leave. In fact, I think he's even managed to convince himself. But it was

82

your choice, wasn't it? You could stay with your husband and four children, or you could live in the sunshine with Tony. You chose the sunshine.

'Even now, you think you have the right to walk in here as if you've never been away. You dump us for the sunshine, then expect to have the red carpet treatment when you deign to visit!'

Colleen opened her mouth to speak but the only sound that emerged was a choked sob. She tried to take a deep breath, but her throat was raw.

She felt like her life was collapsing around her and she was incapable of doing anything to stop it. First Tony, now Sarah . . .

She felt the sting of tears and dabbed quickly at her eyes, but the action only stimulated more tears.

'Mum?' Sarah's voice suddenly sounded young and uncertain.

'I had no idea.' Huge wracking sobs shook Colleen's body and she was unable to stop the tears pouring down her face. 'Oh Sarah, what am I going to do?'

Sarah crossed the room in three quick strides, dropped to her knees and threw her arms around her mother . . .

4

Sarah had never seen her mother cry. Now, holding Colleen close and failing to find words that might halt the flow of tears, she wondered if she knew her mother at all.

'Mum, I'm sorry. I didn't mean any of those things, not really.'

'Yes, you did, love.' Colleen managed a wobbly smile and rubbed at her tear-stained face with her hands. As this didn't improve matters, she reached for her bag and took out a tissue. 'It's not just you, Sarah.' She dabbed at her face before confessing, 'Everything's going wrong between Tony and me.'

'You and Tony?' Sarah frowned, not understanding. 'How do you mean, going wrong?'

'I don't know but it frightens me,' Colleen answered shakily.

'What exactly is happening?'

'He's grown so remote.' Colleen took a calming breath. 'The more I ask what the problem is, the more he insists that nothing's wrong. And the more irritable he becomes. I've imagined all sorts of things. I've thought he might not love me anymore, that he's found someone else.'

'Mum, no,' Sarah said urgently. 'Tony loves you, everyone knows that.'

'That's what I keep telling myself.' She tried to smile and failed. 'But he barely speaks to me and, when he does, it's to tell me not to fuss. Usually, he likes my company but not this time.' She swallowed. 'He didn't want me to come to England.'

Sarah sat on the floor, close to where Colleen sat on the sofa. Try as she might, and Sarah had tried hard over the years, she hadn't been able to find anything in Tony to feed any resentment. He was like an open book, one of those frank, honest, friendly people it was impossible to dislike.

'Sorry, love.' Colleen squeezed her daughter's shoulder. 'I didn't mean to burden you with all this. I came here thinking it would give Tony and me a breathing space and I thought it would be a nice surprise for you all.'

'And I threw a tantrum.' She grimaced. 'I really am sorry, Mum.'

'Perhaps you have every right to feel as you do,' Colleen murmured sadly.

Sarah's feelings were so confused she no longer knew how she felt.

'Will you tell me about it?' she asked.

'I'm not sure if I can, without sounding as if I'm blaming your dad, and it wasn't his fault. It wasn't anyone's fault. Your father is a marvellous man, Sarah, and I have a great deal of admiration and respect for him. I just wasn't the right woman for him.

'I'd been unhappy for a long time but I expect we could have drifted on for a while. Then I met Tony and fell in love with him. I couldn't stay, Sarah. It wouldn't have been fair to your father, or to you children.

'But don't ever think it was an easy decision,' she added quickly. 'When I first thought of marrying Tony, I planned to take you with me. I hadn't contemplated a life without you. It was what I wanted and it was what Tony wanted.

'Your dad made me face facts, though. I was being selfish, Sarah. I couldn't drag you off to another country and a completely different life.'

Sarah touched her mother's arm.

'Dad's told me.' But Sarah had never considered her mother's feelings before.

'It wasn't easy for anyone,' Colleen admitted with a sigh. 'I knew Ralph was more than capable of taking care of you, but I knew it wouldn't be easy for him.

Then there was Tony, trying to cope with a wife whose thoughts were always with her children.

'But,' she added firmly, 'I don't believe the alternative would have been better, I honestly don't, Sarah. I hate living so far away from you, and I hate having to rely on Ralph for information. Your dad and I have a good relationship, but everything's second-hand. I don't share things with you, with any of you, and that hurts.'

She held Sarah's hand between her own.

'I might not have been much of a mother, Sarah, but I have always loved you. All of you.'

Sharp tears stung Sarah's eyes.

'Perhaps we could try harder,' she suggested, her voice hoarse.

'I'm sure we could,' Colleen agreed gently.

A car pulled into the drive and Sarah blinked away her tears.

'That'll be Andy.' She walked over to the window, but it wasn't her brother, it was Ben. 'Oh, heavens, I forgot I was supposed to be going out with Ben.'

'Who's Ben? A boyfriend?'

'He is not!' Sarah answered a little too quickly. 'I only met him a couple of weeks ago.' With a wry smile, she added, 'I only agreed to go out with him because his bare-faced cheek caught me off guard.'

She ran to the door and opened it before he had chance to ring the bell.

'Sorry, Ben, I forgot we were going out.' She stepped back to let him in. 'Come and meet my mother while I get changed.'

As Sarah introduced them, she wondered what her mother saw when she looked at Ben. Sarah saw a handsome, self-confident young man with light brown hair, an enormous smile and mischievous green eyes. A young man, she suspected, who flirted with girls for the sheer fun of it. She would have liked her mother's opinion.

'I'll go and change,' she told them. 'I won't be a minute.'

As she went upstairs to her room, she could hear the murmur of their voices. She was brushing her hair when she heard Andy's noisy arrival. She was pleased her brother was home; she hadn't wanted to leave Colleen alone.

After a few words with Andy, and a promise to Colleen that they would talk in the morning, Sarah left with Ben.

He had tickets for a concert but, as he drove them away from the house, Sarah knew she should have told him to take someone else. She would be poor company.

For years she'd longed to tell her mother exactly what she thought of her. Now she had, she felt thoroughly depressed. She had behaved like a spoilt, selfish brat.

'What's wrong?' Ben asked curiously.

She knew he wouldn't understand and was amazed to hear herself confiding in him. She needed to talk and he was there, she supposed.

It all came pouring out, the resentment she'd felt since Colleen first went to America, and the stupid things she'd said earlier.

'You're obviously forgiven,' he said when she'd finished. 'Your mum spent fifteen minutes telling me how beautiful and talented you are. Not that I needed convincing, of course.'

She smiled and he added gently, 'She's very proud of you. She loves you very much, Sarah.'

'I know.'

She bit her lip and stared at the view moving past the window.

Ben did understand, and the knowledge surprised her. But then, everything about Ben surprised her.

He worked for the Inland Revenue, which is where they'd met. Shocked by the arrival of her tax return, and knowing she didn't have a hope of paying her income tax without her dad's help, she'd gone to the tax office to pick up a couple of 'helpful leaflets'.

Ben had asked about her business and given her all the relevant information.

'It's quite complicated,' he'd said, green eyes twinkling wickedly. 'How about we discuss it over dinner tonight?'

Sarah was so taken aback that, within seconds, he had her name, address, phone number and a promise to be ready at seven-thirty.

Admittedly, dinner had been a highly enjoyable affair but they hadn't even mentioned income tax — Ben had been too busy persuading her to go to the cinema on the following Friday. The day after that, he told her he had two tickets for tonight's concert . . .

For some reason, she found it impossible to say no to him.

'It's our third date,' he broke into her thoughts.

'So?'

'Surely I get to kiss you on our third date?'

'You get to kiss me,' she told him, unable to suppress a burst of laughter, 'when I'm good and ready . . . '

★ ★ ★

Megan had spent most of the day, as well as a large part of a sleepless night, wondering how she should behave towards Hans. She was none the wiser.

He had kissed her before, many times, but always as a friend, and she had known, or assumed, that it meant nothing to him. Those had been kisses from an exuberant acquaintance, the blond tornado as Flora called him, but yesterday's kiss had taken her completely by surprise. Every time she tried to analyse her feelings, she got no further than remembering the myriad sensations his kiss had caused . . .

She was still pondering the problem when she and Hans stepped out of the house, on their way to dinner, but it was suddenly forgotten.

'What the — '

Being dragged up the path, by the biggest, ugliest excuse for a dog Megan had ever seen, was Joy.

'Oh, no,' Megan said firmly, ignoring Hans' deep rumble of laughter.

'I thought you were going out to dinner,' Joy admitted sheepishly.

The dog, big, brown and shaggy, flopped into an inelegant sitting position and began

91

wagging a tail that could wreck a house in minutes.

'We are,' Megan replied, 'and if you think that animal is putting one paw — '

'But, Mum, he'll be no trouble and it's only for a week.' Joy's voice was pleading earnestly. 'He's got nowhere else to go. No one wants him because he's old and a bit on the big side.'

'A bit on the big side? I've seen smaller donkeys!'

'But if we don't give him a home, he'll have to be put down.'

Despite Joy's pathetic expression — the same expression she'd worn when she'd brought home Sugar and Spice, the cats, and Spike, the hedgehog, Megan didn't believe her story for a moment. Brenda, the woman in charge of the rescue kennels, was as big a softie as Joy.

The dog made a dash for the house, nearly knocking Megan over in the process. Joy was still clinging to his lead and had to follow in his wake.

Megan, suspecting she was on the losing side, and Hans, still grinning, followed.

'His name's Rebel,' Joy told them.

'I wonder why,' Megan said dryly.

'Hans — ' Joy slipped her arm through his — 'you wouldn't let Mum turn a defenceless creature onto the streets, would you?'

'I refuse to become involved,' he insisted with amusement. With a wink for Joy's benefit, he gave a casual shrug. 'It's your mother's home, Joy. If she's not prepared to offer the unfortunate animal a home, there's nothing I can do.'

'Unfortunate animal?' Megan scoffed.

Rebel, she noticed, was currently eyeing up the sofa, as if trying to decide whether or not the cushions had been placed there for his personal comfort.

'A week, you said?' she asked Joy and Joy, smelling victory, nodded.

'I said we'd take him on a week's trial. If it doesn't work out — ' She left the sentence unfinished.

'Flora's at work,' Megan reminded her daughter, 'Daisy's in Manchester, and you're at school. Who,' she asked pointedly, 'is going to exercise him?'

'I will,' Joy promised. 'Before school and afterwards. And on Saturdays, I'll take him to the kennels with me.'

'But where will he sleep?' Megan demanded.

'Anywhere he likes, I should imagine,' Hans said with a chuckle.

On that highly probable note, Megan and Hans left the house for the second time.

Megan supposed she should have known

that sharing a home with only two cats and a hedgehog was too good to last. She wouldn't have minded if Joy had brought them a hamster, a guinea pig or a rabbit, but that dog needed a paddock, not a bed.

'Thank you for your support, Hans.' Megan tried to scowl at him as she fastened her seat belt but his enormous grin didn't make it easy.

'What could I do,' he demanded on a burst of laughter, 'when it was obvious to anyone that you wouldn't turn him away?'

'You think I'm too soft?'

'No.' He started the engine, but didn't drive off. Instead, he turned to smile at her. 'I think you have a very big heart. I think you're wonderful.'

'Stupid is probably a more accurate description.' Megan, blushing furiously, pretended to adjust her seat belt as Hans finally drove them away from the house.

She tried to think about Rebel, the new arrival in their home, and about how she could get rid of him, but all she could think of was the way Joy had appealed to Hans' better nature. Almost without Megan noticing, Hans had found his way into her children's hearts.

Megan knew, too, that Joy had hoped to sneak Rebel into the house while she was out, knowing that an evening with Hans would have put her in a very amenable mood . . .

They spent the evening at their favourite restaurant. Megan had come to think of it as 'their place', and they were shown to what she thought of as 'their table'.

She took a long time to choose from the menu; she couldn't concentrate on food.

'I need to talk to you,' Hans interrupted her thoughts.

Megan's heart raced wildly, a mixture of excitement and panic.

'Oh?'

'Yes. Two things. Do you remember me mentioning Doug Nicolson?'

She had to swallow her disappointment.

'Vaguely. He's a friend of yours, isn't he? In the publishing business?'

'He's behind *En Passant*, the glossy monthly magazine.'

'Flora kept pestering you to put in a good word for her,' Megan remembered with a smile.

'That's right.' He chose his next words with care. 'I mentioned Flora to him a few months ago and, since then, he's been having a look at her work. He's impressed, Megan. So impressed he'd like to see her with a view to offering her a position on the magazine.'

'Freelance?' Megan was amazed.

'No. Staff.'

'In London?'

'Yes.' Hans knew exactly what she was thinking. 'Obviously, if he offers her a job, and if she accepts, which I feel sure she will, it will mean a move to London. If you're really unhappy with the idea, I can — '

'Oh, no,' Megan interrupted him, 'I would never forgive myself.'

'Then I'll tell Doug to get in touch with her?'

'Yes.' She nodded. 'I'll be suitably proud and excited for her, and I'll worry in silence.'

Hans laughed.

'Don't. Flora's more than capable of taking care of herself.'

'I know,' Megan agreed, a little wistfully.

They paused for a moment as a waiter placed two cups of coffee on the table.

'You said you wanted to talk about two things?' she asked and Hans nodded.

'It's about the amount of time I'm spending in the UK,' he explained carefully. 'I'm thinking of buying a property here. Or in London at least. What do you think?'

'Well — ' Megan's heart raced. 'If you think you'll have plenty of business here in the future, then it might be more practical, yes.'

'Megan!' He reached across the table and

covered her hand with his. 'The amount of time I'm spending here has little to do with business and you know it.'

'I don't know it, Hans.' She could feel her face redden.

'Yesterday, I kissed you,' he said gently, 'and you've been in shock ever since. Was it really such a surprise?'

'Yes,' she answered truthfully. 'Flora's teased me relentlessly for months. Jackie has, too. But Richard was my first serious boyfriend,' she explained, 'and when he died, it was a case of if I couldn't have him, I didn't want anyone. Since then, I've been too involved with the children to think about another relationship. Besides,' she added dryly, 'ageing mothers of three aren't in great demand.'

'Megan, you're priceless.' Hans laughed.

'Whenever anyone said anything, I deliberately pushed the thought aside,' she confessed. 'I was too frightened to think about it in case they were wrong.'

'And now you know they were right?' he asked, his blue eyes filled with uncertainties. 'You're not planning to go prim on me and suggest we don't see so much of each other in future?'

'No!' He looked so serious that Megan was horrified. 'Of course not. I'm saying that when you kissed me, you took me by surprise, Hans. I'm not saying I didn't like it.'

'You did like it?'

'Very much,' she answered softly . . .

Soon afterwards, Hans paid the bill and, as it was such a pleasant evening, they decided to walk for a while. Hans took her arm and pulled it through his. She tried to forget that he was returning to Germany in the morning.

She wasn't sure which surprised her most, that Hans could be attracted to her, or that she could feel as she did.

Like many teenagers, she had devoted much time to searching for Mr Right and when she found him, in the shape of Richard, she had thought that was it. She had known the search was over, and had dreamed of the two of them growing old together. Since Richard's death, she hadn't even dreamed about falling in love again. She had a known a deep and true love once. Expecting to find it again seemed almost greedy . . .

'I should be back in the UK after the weekend,' Hans said. 'Shall we look for a suitable property?'

'You want me to help?'

'Of course. Who else?' He stopped walking and put a gentle finger beneath her chin. 'I want to become involved in your life, and I want you involved in mine.' He grasped her hands and held them tight. 'I'm trying to say I love you, Megan.'

His words thrilled her and she struggled to think coherently.

'It's very sudden, Hans.'

'Not for me. Is there a chance you could fall in love with me?'

'Every chance,' she whispered.

They had reached his car but instead of opening the door, Hans wrapped his arms around her.

'I've never felt like this before,' he confessed. 'When I was younger, I imagined myself in love several times, but my ambition always got in the way. Now, none of that seems important. All that matters to me is your happiness.'

And this time, Megan would have been surprised — and disappointed — if he *hadn't* kissed her . . .

* * *

The following day, Megan woke to grey skies and the first of the day's many showers. She tried to recapture the magic of Hans' kiss, but Hans was on a plane bound for Germany and the day stretched emptily ahead.

99

The girls were all busy. Megan would have sought out Jackie, her best friend, but it was Jackie's day to visit her mother.

In any case, Megan wasn't sure that she wanted to confide in anyone just yet. What had felt wonderfully right last night seemed a little impulsive this morning.

Doubts crowded in and she wished she could hear the sound of Hans' voice . . .

To clear her head, she decided to take Rebel for a long walk.

Surprisingly, he was very well behaved. Apart from a couple of occasions when he forgot he was on his lead and tried to chase leaves blowing in the breeze, Megan enjoyed his company. She hadn't been won over — she still didn't want a dog in the house, especially an enormous one like Rebel who needed too much exercise, too much food, and too much grooming — but she had to admit that he did have his good points.

As the house came in view, she saw a car similar to Ralph Pettifer's parked outside.

'My car wouldn't start,' Flora greeted her, 'so Ralph offered to bring me home. The garage is sending someone out in the morning so I'm hoping it's nothing too expensive. Andy had a look but he couldn't find anything wrong with it.'

'That was her first mistake,' Ralph told

Megan with amusement.

'I'll get another cup,' Flora said, adding, 'Come on, Rebel. I bought you some chocolate drops today.'

'Oh, great. You should see how good he is at catching them . . . ' Joy followed her sister.

'Thanks for bringing Flora home, Ralph,' Megan said. 'You should have let her call me. I could easily have come for her.'

'It was no trouble. Sarah was going to bring her but her boyfriend turned up unexpectedly. From what I gather, everything Ben does is unexpected.'

Smiling, Megan poured them coffee.

'Has Colleen gone back to London?'

'Yesterday.' He nodded. 'She wasn't sure when they were going back to California so she might pay another visit . . . '

'Hey, look!'

Joy and Flora returned to give a demonstration of Rebel's remarkable ability.

'With a mouth that size,' Ralph pointed out, 'I'd be more impressed if he didn't catch them.'

As they drank coffee, there wasn't a pause in the conversation. Again, Megan was struck by how easily Ralph fitted in. She supposed his circumstances were very similar, though. Like her, he was used to the irreverent humour that came from sharing a home with young adults.

'If you can take me to work in the morning, Mum,' Flora said thoughtfully, 'I'll get a bus to pick up my car in the afternoon. But if it's not fixed — ' she gave Megan an appealing look ' — can I borrow yours tomorrow night? I'm working. I have to sit through 'The Mikado', of all things.'

'Lucky you,' Megan exclaimed, and Flora rolled her eyes.

'Lucky? Oh, please. Why they're letting me cover it, I can't imagine. I won't know if it's good, bad or indifferent.'

'You'll enjoy it,' Megan told her, smiling as she remembered, 'although I once went to a production with your dad and he slept right through it.'

'I don't blame him.' Flora chuckled.

'Colleen and I went,' Ralph remembered, 'but as the lights went down, Mark decided it was time to enter the world.'

'Then allow me to make you both very happy.' Flora grabbed her bag and pulled out a notepad, several pens, three hairbrushes and, finally, a very crumpled envelope. 'Two complimentary tickets!'

She took the tickets from the envelope and flattened them across her knee.

'They're a bit the worse for wear,' she said,

'but I didn't expect to be able to do anything with them. And they're for Friday night. Any takers?'

'Megan?' Ralph asked.

'Well — '

'I'm free,' he said. 'In fact, I have the luxury of a whole weekend off. If you'd like to go, I could pick you up.'

'Good idea,' Flora agreed. 'It would be silly to take two cars. So can I borrow your car tomorrow night, Mum, if mine's not fixed?'

'Well, yes,' Megan answered, a little hesitantly.

* * *

Colleen had never liked hotel rooms. Their temporary nature unsettled her.

Tony was lying beside her, giving every indication of being asleep, but she wasn't convinced. They'd had a long, tiring day — she'd done a round of the galleries and Tony had attended a business meeting — followed by an evening with Mark and Carol. It was late when they finally got to bed and they should have been asleep an hour ago.

Colleen, however, was too restless to sleep. It had been wonderful to see Mark again.

103

From the moment he was born, he'd been the image of Ralph, and now he resembled his father more than ever. Even his mannerisms were the same. Colleen found it impossible to look at Mark without remembering the young medical student she had married all those years ago.

She'd seen echoes of herself in his girlfriend, too. Carol was heading for a promising career in law, whereas Colleen had studied history, but the similarities were there. Colleen, of course, had been quick — too quick — to abandon all thoughts of a career when she fell in love with Ralph. She hoped Carol didn't make the same mistake. In Colleen's experience, new doctors were too busy for marriage and their wives were best advised to have a fulfilling career of their own.

Such forward thinking made her smile to herself. She doubted if Mark had spared a thought for marriage.

Her thoughts drifted to Sarah and she felt tears spring to her eyes. They had parted on good terms but that didn't erase the feelings Sarah had harboured for so long. Colleen closed her eyes on the tears. Wrongs could be put right, she told herself. It wasn't too late.

They'd had a good long chat about Ben.

Colleen had thought him far too attractive for his own good, but she'd liked him. Sarah, though, was being very cautious, calling him 'a dreadful flirt with an eye for a pretty face'. How she could be so sure, after only three dates, Colleen didn't know. She hoped the divorce hadn't made her daughter cynical.

Andy certainly wasn't cynical, she thought with an inner smile. He was in love and he wanted the whole world to know it.

And Jack. He was the same gentle, loving soul he had always been.

Colleen knew she was very lucky to have four wonderful children. She knew it, even as the tears slid onto her cheeks . . .

She wasn't sure what woke her. It might have been a dream, a sound, or simply reaching out for Tony and finding herself alone in the bed.

Glowing red numerals told her it was twenty past three. She sat up quickly and snapped on the bedside light.

'Tony?'

He was sitting by the window, staring out across the city.

'Go back to sleep, Colleen.'

Her dressing gown was still lying at the foot of the bed and she slipped it on. She ignored Tony's sigh as she pulled up a chair and placed it next to him. The room wasn't cold but she pulled her dressing gown tight as she sat down.

All her worries gathered in the pit of her stomach as she looked at him. She hadn't told Sarah her main fear, that he might be seriously ill.

The light was dim but she could see the shadows around his eyes. He'd lost weight recently. His face was thin and drawn, and beneath the tan of the Californian sun his skin was a tense shade of grey. He was fifty-two years old and, for the first time, Colleen thought he looked every day of it — and more.

'You look awful.'

'Don't start, Colleen. Not now.' He didn't even look at her, he just stared at the city's lights.

'I am going to start, Tony, and I'm not going to stop until you tell me exactly what the problem is. You can't keep fobbing me off, telling me everything's fine. I know you too well.'

He turned to look at her, but offered no explanation.

'Tony, I have a right to know what's happening. I'm your wife. I love you.'

'Do you?' he asked quietly.

'You need to ask?' she cried. 'How can

you? You know I love you. I gave up my children for you!'

'And I gave up my children for you!' With a groan, he covered his face with his hands. 'Colleen — ' He reached out for her hand, but she was standing at the window, her back to him and her arms tightly folded.

He stood behind her and wrapped his arms around her waist.

'What are we doing to each other, darling?'

They were hurting each other. He was right, he did give up all hopes of having children of his own when he married her. Colleen had told him that she wouldn't, *couldn't*, have more children. She would have felt she was trying to replace her own. And she had been frightened that she might not be able to love more children.

'You know I didn't mean that,' Tony said gently. 'All I wanted was you, Colleen. Nothing else was important.'

'And now?'

'Nothing's changed.'

'Everything's changed!' She spun round to face him. 'We used to talk, Tony. We used to share things. For better or worse, remember?'

'I remember.'

He took her hand and led her back to the chairs. He sat down and pulled her down to sit on his lap. 'I remember the man you married — just,' he said quietly. 'A pushy, ambitious man who'd taken the advertising world by storm. People said I had the Midas touch,' he recalled grimly. 'You married a man capable of giving you a very comfortable lifestyle, Colleen. You could cross the Atlantic whenever you chose, put your children on a plane whenever you chose . . . '

'More importantly,' she reminded him, 'I married a man who shared his every thought with me.'

'What if things had been different?' he asked softly, ignoring that. 'What if I hadn't been so lucky? In the early days, I took a lot of gambles, Colleen. What if they hadn't paid off?'

'We would have lived in a smaller house and the children would have slept on the floor. Like a lot of other wives, I would have got a job somewhere. We would have scrimped and saved for cars, holidays.' She shrugged. 'Financially, we've had an easy life, Tony, but so what?'

A sudden thought struck her.

'Is the company in trouble?'

His hands were trembling and she clasped them in her own.

'Is that it, Tony? Is the company in trouble?'

He nodded and Colleen saw the shimmer of tears in his eyes. He pulled her close, so that his voice was muffled by her hair.

'Oh, Colleen, I am so sorry. I've tried everything, darling, I promise you. I can't think of anything else that might save it.' His voice broke and it was a moment before he spoke again. 'Soon, there won't be a company to save.'

5

Orange streetlights gave the car's interior a cosy glow but Megan didn't feel cosy. She'd been too enthralled in a breathtaking performance of 'The Mikado' to do anything other than enjoy herself but now, as Ralph drove her home, everything felt wrong.

This wasn't a date, she reminded herself for the hundredth time. Flora had been right; it would have been a waste if those two seats had been empty.

Megan supposed her social life had revolved around her children for so long that she was out of touch. She was also very old-fashioned, she decided.

It was foolish, she knew it was, but she felt that by being with Ralph, she was being disloyal to Hans. It didn't seem right to tell Hans she was a step away from falling in love with him one minute, then enjoy an evening with Ralph the next. Megan knew there was nothing vaguely romantic about this evening, just as Ralph knew it, just as Hans would, but still it didn't feel right to be out with an attractive man. And there was no getting away from the fact that Ralph was an extremely attractive man . . .

'Is Daisy coming home for the weekend?' he asked as he brought the car to a stop in front of a set of lights.

'Yes. Andy's driving down with her in the morning. Didn't you know?'

'No,' he replied with a wry smile. 'I've learned to expect Andy when I see him.'

Megan knew exactly what he meant. She, too, was finding it increasingly difficult to keep tabs on her daughters' whereabouts.

'They're taking the train to London on Sunday, I gather,' Megan explained, 'to see Colleen and Tony.'

'Really?' He drove them away from the traffic lights. 'They grow up very quickly, don't they?' he added a touch wistfully.

'They do,' she agreed softly. 'Under your feet one minute, gone the next.'

He nodded.

'Years ago, there were times when I longed for them to be grown up and independent. Now . . . ' He shrugged.

'I know,' Megan agreed. 'I dread the thought of an empty house.'

'Me, too.'

He took the road out of the city and Megan smiled.

'I can't see any of them — yours or mine — going far away or staying away.

111

In any case,' she added, 'loneliness is a state of mind, isn't it? It doesn't matter a jot if the house is full or empty. There have been times,' she admitted, 'when I've had three lovely children making demands on my time and been almost overwhelmed with loneliness.'

'When Richard died?' he guessed and she nodded.

'Did you ever feel like that? When Colleen left?'

'Many times,' he confessed. 'I would come home to four noisy children and the house would feel unbearably empty.'

He gave her a brief sideways glance. 'Much more of this,' he said with a wry smile, 'and I shall have to prescribe us something.'

'Sorry.' She laughed.

Minutes later Ralph turned the car into her drive. He kept the headlights on so she could see the door but he didn't switch off the engine and she was pleased. If he had, she wouldn't have known whether to ask him in or not.

'I've enjoyed this evening, Megan,' he said. 'Thank you for coming.'

'Oh — no. I enjoyed it, too. Thank you.' She was fumbling with her seat-belt and he had to help her unfasten it. 'Thank you,' she said breathlessly when she was finally free. 'Well, goodnight, Ralph. And thanks again.'

'Goodnight, Megan.'

Megan got out of the car, walked up the path, opened the front door and turned to wave to him. Then she let herself inside and leaned back against the door as she listened to the sound of his car driving away.

She desperately needed to talk to Hans. When she was with him, everything made sense. Away from him, she was an emotional mess.

It was late, too late to call Hans, so she went to bed and spent a long, sleepless night trying to get her feelings into some sort of order. When she was with him, she thought she was in love. Away from him, her feelings seemed very juvenile. Did she love Hans? Or was it the *idea* of falling in love, and the thrill that came with it, she found so exciting?

For a moment, she envied Daisy. Her daughter might be on the verge of making the biggest mistake of her life but at least she was sure of her feelings . . .

Megan woke early. She went quietly down the stairs, not wanting to wake Flora or Joy, and rang Hans' number.

It rang out, repeatedly, and she was about to replace the receiver when a woman answered. Megan tried to ignore the tight knot in her stomach that the female voice caused and asked to speak to Hans.

'*Wer ist da?*' The woman sounded hesitant, as if not sure whether to get Hans or not.

'Megan — er — Megan Somerby,' she answered.

There was a clatter as the receiver was put on a table, then silence. Megan waited. It was a long time before she heard noises, then the clatter of the receiver being picked up.

'Megan, my darling girl!' Hans' voice boomed out. 'What a perfect way to start the day!'

She laughed at his exuberance and a rush of some emotion acutely close to love brought tears to her eyes.

'Is this call business or social?' he asked.

'Social. I just wondered if you knew when you'd be back in England.'

'You're missing me. Yes?'

'Yes,' she answered truthfully and he gave a delighted chuckle.

'I'm glad to hear it. All being well, I shall be with you on Wednesday.'

They talked for a few minutes but all the while Megan's mind was on other things.

'Hans?'

'Yes?'

'Oh — no.' She felt ridiculous, like a moonstruck adolescent. 'It's nothing.'

114

'Megan?' he prompted.

'I was curious,' she admitted hesitantly, 'about the woman who answered your phone.'

'My sister-in-law,' he answered with a deep rumble of laughter. 'She and my brother are staying for a couple of days. They're taking an old wooden chest off my hands — an ugly thing that's been in the family for years that I shall be glad to get rid of. When you called, Harald and I were struggling to get it down the stairs.'

Megan was ridiculously pleased.

'I'm glad you were jealous, though,' Hans added with amusement.

'I was nothing of the sort!' But she was laughing happily when she replaced the receiver.

★ ★ ★

'Well?' Colleen asked as she showed Tony their new hotel room.

He looked at the bed in the centre of the small room, then back at Colleen.

'It's awful.' As if trying to find something to commend it, even something as simple as a view, he walked to the window and looked out at rows of Victorian buildings. 'Whatever possessed you?' he asked in amazement.

'It is not awful,' Colleen argued. 'It's very — cosy. And the menu is excellent, I looked it up in my guide book.'

'Cosy?' he muttered. 'There isn't room to — ' But words failed him.

'We don't need room, Tony. All we need is a decent breakfast and evening meal, if we're not out that is, and a bed.' She threw herself down on the bed and grinned as several springs protested loudly. 'OK, so the bed leaves a little to be desired. But we were rattling around in that suite with its stunning view — for what? It was a waste of money, Tony.'

Tony expelled his breath on a weary sigh and sat on the edge of the bed. 'So you think that by checking us out and moving us here, you've solved all our problems?'

'Of course not.' The savings on the hotel were peanuts, she knew that. 'But every little helps. Come here,' she said, patting the bed beside her.

With a great deal of reluctance, and a huge scowl as the bed springs burst into tuneless song, he stretched out beside her. Physically he was closer, but emotionally he was as distant as ever. He lay on his back with his hands linked beneath his head.

'I think it's a lovely room,' Colleen said, gazing fondly at the rose covered wallpaper and thick velvet curtains.

'You think everything is lovely at the moment,' he replied dryly.

'I'm happy,' she agreed with satisfaction. 'Probably happier than I've ever been.'

'Everything's falling apart around us, Colleen. How *can* you be happy?'

'Easily.' She propped herself up on her elbow and gazed at his frowning face.

'I thought you'd met someone else,' she confessed. 'And in my darkest moments, I thought you were ill — seriously ill, Tony. For the last few weeks, no, months, I've been worried to death. I had no idea what the problem was but I was convinced that, one way or another, I was losing you. To find that our only problems are financial ones is bliss. It's only money, Tony, that's all.'

'Only money,' he echoed with a shake of his head.

Colleen watched Tony carefully. Of course it wasn't only money to Tony. The company had been his life for years. He'd founded it, nurtured it, and watched it grow. It would be more than he could bear to watch it crumble to nothing . . .

'Why didn't you tell me?' she asked quietly.

'There was no point worrying you,' he replied, 'and I thought — hoped — things would improve. It's hard to believe that one ad campaign can cause so much damage.'

'Vic Douglas's ad campaign?' she guessed and he nodded.

Ironically, Vic Douglas and his innovative ideas had been on the wanted list of most advertising firms when a disagreement had him breaking up the prestigious Walker and Douglas partnership. Tony had considered himself lucky to get him.

Not surprisingly, Vic had been put in charge of a major new campaign. What Tony hadn't known and what his client hadn't known was that Vic was very bitter. The new campaign would have been a great success if Vic's ideas hadn't been 'stolen' from Walker and Douglas.

The law suit that followed had been long and fierce with Tony, eventually, being forced to make a huge financial settlement.

But the settlement had been made over a year ago and Vic was long gone. Colleen had thought it was over.

She reached for Tony's hand and held it in her own.

'What you've done before, Tony, you can do again,' she said urgently. 'You started the company from nothing, you can get it back on its feet again.'

'No.' He shook his head and sighed. 'We

lost all our major clients while we were battling it out with the lawyers. I suppose that was only to be expected. People lose faith, Colleen, and to get their attention back, we need to pull off something big.

To pull off something big, however, we need important clients. It's Catch 22.'

They were silent for a moment before Colleen spoke.

'What's your biggest fear?' she asked curiously.

He didn't answer for a moment.

'That instead of cutting our losses while I still can,' he said at length, 'I shall cling on until we don't have a cent. I worry that you'll grow tired of living a life of poverty and — ' he scowled as the bed creaked ' — and head for pastures new.'

'Tony!' His words hurt and she spoke sharply. 'You think I married you for your bank balance? For your business acumen?'

'No, of course not,' he answered with a frown.

'Then what difference will it make if we're penniless?' she demanded. 'I love you, Tony!'

He increased his grip on her fingers.

'I know that but — '

'But what?'

'It will make life — difficult for you,'

119

he said quietly. 'You in one country, your children in another.'

She could see there was no point in reasoning with him. He looked awful, a man haunted day and night by his worries, and until he could start to relax, he would be no use to the company — or to himself.

She moved closer and it sounded as if sixteen trampolinists were trying out the bed.

'Do you think you'll be able to manage a smile tomorrow?' she asked lightly. 'Andy and Daisy are coming — remember? If you walk around with a face like a wet weekend, you'll put the poor kids off marriage for life.'

'That probably wouldn't be a bad thing,' he retorted with a ghost of a smile.

'What time are they arriving?'

'I said we'd meet them at St Pancras at quarter to ten.' She smiled happily. 'I can't wait to meet Daisy. She must be very special, don't you think?'

'She'll need to be,' he teased, 'if she's planning to spend the rest of her life with Andy.'

Colleen laughed. She had to admit that Andy's practical jokes could drive anyone to the limits of their patience.

'I hope she's the sensible, down-to-earth

type,' Tony mused, 'because Andy isn't.'

'He can be when he wants to be,' she answered seriously. 'And for Daisy, I'm sure he'll want to be. You only have to hear him talk about her to know how much he loves her. Ralph has his doubts, I know, but Andy is very serious about Daisy. And about marriage and all it entails. I wonder what she's like.'

'You've been wondering what she's like for ages,' Tony reminded her with a chuckle. 'You'll have to be patient. You'll see for yourself in the — ' He groaned as the bed springs played a discordant tune. 'This bed has a mind of its own.' He grinned suddenly. 'Unless we spend the night on the floor, my love, we're going to get some very strange looks when we go down for breakfast. I don't think we can pass as honeymooners, do you?'

They collapsed in a fit of uncontrollable giggles. The sound of squealing springs was deafening.

* * *

Andy gazed at Daisy as the train rushed them towards Leicester. She was sitting sideways in her seat, with her back resting against the window and her feet stretched out across his lap. Her eyes were closed but he knew she wasn't sleeping. He hoped she was relaxing — at last.

They'd had an enjoyable day with Colleen and Tony, and it hadn't taken Daisy long to realise that her many fears had been groundless. Andy had spent the week telling her they were groundless but Daisy hadn't been convinced. She'd been expecting more opposition to their marriage and he could only sympathise.

Colleen had taken to her future daughter-in-law immediately, however, just as Andy had known she would.

Daisy opened her eyes and smiled when she found him watching her.

'What are you thinking?'

'That I love you, Daisy Somerby.'

'You would say that.' She grinned at him. 'But as I happen to love you, too, I'll let you off.' She wriggled her feet into a more comfortable position. 'Your mum's really nice, isn't she?'

'Don't sound so surprised,' he retorted with a laugh.

'I'm not. It's just that I thought she'd spend the day telling us that no one under the age of thirty should consider marriage, or that we're too childish to know what we're doing, or that we should trying living together and find out what marriage is really like. But she didn't say any of that. She even asked me what we wanted for a wedding present.'

'Oh? What did you say?'

'I didn't say anything,' Daisy admitted with a laugh. 'I haven't thought that far ahead. She said we ought to think about whether we wanted something to celebrate our marriage, like a good honeymoon, or something practical, like a washing machine.'

'Forget the washing machine,' he replied easily. 'We'll have a month in Tahiti.'

'Fine,' Daisy said. 'So long as you're doing the washing.'

'You think I couldn't?'

'I *know* you couldn't!' She spluttered with laughter.

She swung her feet off him, twisted in her seat, and lifted his arm to put it around her shoulders.

'This job you're going after,' she said slowly. 'The more I think about it, Andy, the less I like it. What if you really hate it?'

'I won't hate it,' he promised.

'You might.' She lifted her worried face to his. 'You wanted to be a cameraman. You wanted to travel. Instead of which, you'll be stuck in a lab processing holiday snaps of Joe Bloggs with his head chopped off.'

'No.' Andy laughed at the description. 'Firstly, I have no wish to travel if it means leaving you behind. Secondly, most people taking holiday snaps of Joe Bloggs with his head chopped off send their films to one of the big mail order labs or drop them off in the High Street. Thirdly, working in a lab has a lot of advantages.'

'Such as?' she asked doubtfully.

'Money for a start,' he reminded her dryly. 'The pay isn't great, admittedly, but it's an ideal job for anyone who wants to do freelance work. I'll know more tomorrow when I've been for the interview, but when I spoke to him on the phone I gathered it was the sort of job where you were either too busy to draw breath or sitting around twiddling your thumbs. There's a lot of very expensive equipment waiting to be used, Daisy. It would be great for a freelance.'

'But I'll feel so guilty,' she said with a groan. 'I'll be doing exactly what I want and you'll be doing a job you hate.'

'I won't hate it,' he said again. 'Nothing's settled, Daisy. I haven't even been offered the job, but if I am, it'll make sense to take it. To keep a roof over our heads, one of us has to work. Agreed?'

'I suppose so,' she admitted reluctantly.

'You're already part-way through your

degree course,' he reminded her, 'so you can't give that up. I, on the other hand, hadn't even got as far as deciding which course to take. I have to get a job, Daisy.'

She sighed and he kissed the top of her head.

'On Friday,' he said, 'we'll go and look at that flat. OK?'

'It'll be expensive,' she warned and he had to laugh.

'Aren't you a regular prophet of doom today!'

'Sorry.' She gave a rueful smile.

He wrapped his arms tight around her as the train sped towards Leicester. Despite his attempt at humour, her pessimistic way of looking at everything was beginning to unnerve him. He could understand up to a point and he knew it was difficult trying to do anything in the face of such strong opposition but still it unnerved him.

She was right about the job; working in a lab wasn't the most exciting of prospects. But if he was offered it, and if he could concentrate on his freelance work, there was always hope for the future. He'd already sold several pictures for calendars and greetings cards.

She was right about the flat, too; it would be expensive. It was currently costing the current tenants, Ian and Mary, every penny they owned, but a lot of improvements had been made over the last year and Ian reckoned that as soon as he and Mary left on Thursday, the rent would be pushed up. Unfurnished accommodation wasn't easy to find, though, and thanks to being friendly with Ian and Mary, he and Daisy had been given first refusal. It was in a good area and close to the university. It would be ideal. Expensive, but ideal.

It wasn't the flat's rent that brought the frown to his face, though, nor was it the job. It was Daisy.

Weeks ago, she'd been as happy and excited as he was. He watched her now, twisting his ring around the third finger of her left hand. Her face, when she lifted it to his, was full of doubts.

'Andy — perhaps I should give up the course and get a job. One day, we'll want children and there won't be much point in my having a good job then, will there?'

'You're not giving up your course,' he said firmly.

'Perhaps — ' her voice faltered 'perhaps we should postpone the wedding until — '

'Until when? No, Daisy!'

'But — '

'But nothing,' he cut her off. 'I love you,

126

Daisy. That's all that matters.'

'I love you, too.'

Her arms snaked around his neck but even as he kissed her, Andy could feel every last one of her doubts . . .

* * *

Flora was beginning to wonder what she was doing in London. Her interview — if it could be called an interview — had been underway for ten minutes and, in that time, Doug Nicolson had taken two telephone calls and was now on his third.

And when he wasn't on the phone, he was glancing at his watch as if he had far more pressing things on his mind. For all the interest he was showing in her, she might not have been in the room.

As a rule, Flora tried not to build up her hopes, but the chance of a job with *En Passant*, the widely-acclaimed, glossy monthly, was the chance of a lifetime.

It had taken her an age to decide what to wear. In the end, she'd dashed out with Sarah and bought this smart, businesslike suit in dark navy. A complete waste of money, she thought grimly, as Doug Nicolson snapped at his caller.

On the train journey this morning, she and

Sarah had conducted half a dozen imaginary interviews and tried to guess the questions she'd have to answer.

Sarah was the only person she'd told about this interview. Flora wasn't a great believer in counting chickens and there was no point telling everyone, and making plans for a future that might never be. They were meeting up with Mark for lunch but he, too, thought that she and Sarah were just on a shopping trip to London.

Flora was beginning to wish she *was* on a shopping trip. More than that, she wished she could walk out the door, walk in again and start this interview afresh.

Doug Nicolson was nothing like the man she'd expected. Firstly, he was much younger than she'd expected. She put him in his mid- to late-thirties, a good fifteen years her senior but still much younger than she'd expected. He was tall and slim, with brown wavy hair that stuck out at all angles, a result of the way he kept pulling his fingers through it when he spoke on the phone. His tie was loose around his neck, his shirt sleeves were rolled back to the elbow and he gave the impression of being the type who thought he could do everyone's job better than they could.

She'd expected the offices to be grander

but this office was a cluttered mess that was badly in need of redecoration . . .

The receiver went down with a bang.

'Right, where were we?' Before Flora could remind him, he looked across the messy desk at her and said, 'I hope you're not expecting any favours, just because you happen to be a friend of Hans.'

She'd thought *he* was supposed to be a friend of Hans, too, but the idea of Hans being friendly with such a rude, irascible man didn't seem possible.

'Not at all.'

'Good, because you won't get any.' He flicked through her portfolio without pausing long enough to actually read any of it.

'On the other hand,' she pointed out, 'I didn't think I was here just because I *am* a friend of Hans. I thought I was being seriously considered for a position on the staff. And I honestly don't see how you can do that if you don't bother to read my work.'

'I've read all I need to,' he answered, either unaware of her simmering anger or choosing to ignore it.

He took a typescript from one of the several piles on his desk and handed her the middle page. 'What's your opinion?'

Flora read the single page. As it was

written in *En Passant*'s very distinctive style, she assumed it was a piece that would soon appear in the magazine. He hadn't given her the first page so she started reading mid-sentence and ended mid-sentence, but it was enough to show her that it was very well written.

'It's very good,' she said, returning the paper to him.

'It is,' he agreed, 'which is why you'll be able to read the full story in next month's issue.' He picked up a pencil and tapped it against the edge of his desk. 'Do you think you could do as well?'

'I could do better!' Flora was bristling with indignation.

His eyes widened slightly at her claim.

'You really think so?'

'No, Mr Nicolson, I *know* so. And so would you if you'd done me the courtesy of reading my work.'

That confounded telephone rang again before he could reply. He told the unknown Annie to put his call on hold 'for a moment' and then turned his attention back to Flora.

He looked vaguely amused as he stood up and held out his hand.

'I think we're about finished,' he told her. 'Thanks for coming. I'll be in touch.'

With her hands shaking from a variety

of raging emotions, Flora picked up her portfolio.

'Thank you for sparing me a few minutes.'

Then, with as much dignity as she could muster, which wasn't a great deal, she walked out of his office and out of the building with her portfolio tucked under her arm.

The streets were busy and she didn't have a clue where she was heading.

She wouldn't have wanted to work for him anyway, she reminded herself with every step. It was only a job after all, and there would be others. Not as good as this one perhaps . . .

It was no use wondering what had gone wrong at her interview, but she couldn't help herself. Perhaps he really had read enough of her work to know she wasn't up to the required standard. Perhaps she'd been fooling herself to think she *was* good enough.

Perhaps it was simply a clash of personalities.

What did it matter, she asked herself impatiently. She'd blown it.

As Flora made her way through the busy streets, she wished she hadn't arranged to have lunch with Sarah and Mark. She wasn't in the mood for bright chit-chat. All she wanted was to go home and forget every moment of this awful day . . .

131

On hearing Flora's car pull into the driveway, Megan jumped out of her chair, went to the kitchen and put the kettle on. She was as nervous as a kitten, which was ridiculous because she didn't even know if Flora had been for an interview.

She suspected she had, though. Flora wouldn't have bought a new suit and worn it for a day round the shops with Sarah. There had to be a far more important reason for today's trip.

'In here, love!' she called out when she heard Flora come into the hall.

She waited for Flora's excited entrance but nothing happened. Slightly concerned, Megan went into the hall.

'Flora?'

'Oh, Mum!' Flora's hands flew to her face and she burst into tears.

'Whatever's happened?' Megan asked anxiously. 'Flora, love, what is it?' Concern turned to alarm as her mind whirled through a million things that could happen to a pretty young girl in the city. 'Come on, Flora. Come and tell me all about it?'

Flora allowed herself to be led into the sitting-room, and threw herself down on the sofa, but it was a couple of minutes before the tears stopped. She brushed the back of her hand across her face in a surprisingly childlike gesture.

'Today has been the worst day of my life,' she said on a sob. 'Everything I ever dreamed of — ' She grabbed a tissue from the box and blew her nose. 'You know Doug Nicolson, Hans' friend?'

Megan nodded and Flora sniffed again.

'And you know I've been trying to persuade Hans to put in a good word for me?'

'Hans told me he'd spoken to him,' Megan admitted.

'He did?' Flora digested this piece of information. 'Well, I went for an interview today.'

'I wondered if you had.' She smiled. 'I didn't think that shopping with Sarah warranted a new suit.'

'You knew? So why didn't you say?'

'Probably the same reason you didn't, love,' Megan said quietly. 'Until you'd been offered a job, there wasn't much to say, was there?'

'That's what I thought.' Flora ran a dejected hand over Rebel's head then fondled his ears. 'It's not that I want to leave home, Mum, it's just that — '

'The best jobs are in London?' Megan suggested, and Flora nodded miserably.

'But neither of us has to worry, I shan't be working in London.' She blew her nose again. 'Not for Doug Nicolson at any rate. I know I shouldn't have built up my hopes but I honestly believed I was good enough.'

'And he said you weren't?' Megan asked gently, her heart aching for poor Flora.

'Not in so many words,' Flora answered. 'He didn't say anything much. Or not to me. He spent most of the time on the phone. And he had the cheek to tell me not to expect any favours, just because I was a friend of Hans. As if I needed any favours! It was so unfair, Mum. He didn't even bother to read my work. He said he'd read as much as he needed to then dismissed me as if I were nothing more than an irritation to him. And I expect I was. I expect he only agreed to see me as a favour to Hans. Although how Hans has a friend like that, I can't imagine. I certainly wouldn't want to work for a man like him.' Threatening tears caused her lower lip to wobble. 'But, oh, I did so want to work on his magazine.'

Megan wished there was something constructive she could say, but she knew there wasn't. She didn't like the idea of Flora living in London, but she certainly didn't want to see her stuck in a job that she'd outgrown. 'There are bound to be other jobs, love.'

'Not that good.'

'There will,' Megan promised. 'And it's only one man's opinion, Flora. Someone else might have thought differently. I'll put the kettle on,' she said, rising to her feet, 'and you can tell me about the rest of the day.

'Did you and Sarah have lunch?'

'Yes, we met up with Mark.'

'He OK?' Megan called from the kitchen.

'Fine.'

'And did Sarah do any shopping?'

'A pair of shoes and a dress.'

Megan fell silent.

It was obvious that Flora wasn't going to be cheered by talking about a day that had been her own personal disaster. She only hoped her daughter would be able to go back to work and put her heart into a job she had hoped to leave . . .

The phone rang and Megan reached out absently for it.

'Hello?'

'May I speak to Flora Somerby, please? My name's Doug Nicolson . . . '

135

6

The restaurant was full, and the murmur of voices, mingled with the occasional sound of laughter, drifted across to Hans and Megan's table.

'You spoil me,' Megan said contentedly as she slipped off her shoes.

'You deserve it.' Hans smiled across the table. 'Especially today,' he added with a slight frown. 'You were looking a little stressed earlier.'

She was forced to laugh at the truth of it.

'You should try living with my three,' she said. 'We seem to be stumbling from one disaster to another at the moment.'

'Where are your three tonight?'

'Flora and Daisy have gone to see a play. It's one of these modern things, something about Romeo and Juliet celebrating the millennium. I gather it's a farce. A crowd of them have gone — Sarah, Flora, Andy and Daisy, Mark, I think, and Ben, Sarah's boyfriend.

'And Joy's at her friend's, supposedly doing some last-minute revising for Monday's exam. It's always the same with Joy,' she continued with amusement. 'She's decided what she wants to do with her life and has written off to find out about training dogs for the disabled. But, because she believes she can train dogs without any qualifications, she doesn't give tuppence for exams. At the last minute, though, the prospect of failing is too much for her pride to bear.' She gave him a rueful smile. 'At least Joy's disasters are no worse than suddenly remembering she has an exam on Monday morning. But the other two — ' She rolled her eyes. 'You should have seen Flora when she came back from her interview with Doug Nicolson.'

'Was it really so bad?' Hans frowned.

The waiter brought their main course to the table and Megan waited until they were alone again.

'According to Flora, it was the worst day of her life.'

'But she is taking the job, isn't she?'

'Oh, yes!'

Megan chuckled at the memory of the cool, composed young girl who spoke to Doug Nicolson when he rang to offer her a job. Having told him, very calmly, that she would consider his offer and let him know by the end of the week, Flora had danced a jig around the kitchen.

'She rang him this morning to accept,' she told Hans. 'She'd already given her notice at the paper, but she seemed to gain satisfaction from making Doug Nicolson wait for her decision.' She frowned slightly. 'She didn't like him at all, Hans.'

'He's a good man,' Hans said slowly. 'He works too hard, which is why he's as successful as he is, and, yes, I suppose he can be a little abrupt at times.'

'Flora could cheerfully have hit him,' Megan went on. 'He warned her not to expect any favours, just because she was a friend of yours. She took it as a personal insult, and was quite rude, I gather. She was furious.'

'I can imagine,' Hans murmured, 'but she'll soon get used to him. And she'll enjoy the work, Megan.'

'I know,' she agreed with a small sigh.

'It's not the other side of the world,' he pointed out knowingly. 'It's a straightforward car journey and less than a couple of hours by train.'

'I know,' she repeated. 'I'll miss her, of course, but I'm pleased she's got the job. She was so upset when she thought she'd messed up the interview.'

They concentrated on their food and Megan realised just how hungry she was.

She'd had a busy day, and had missed lunch.

'Has Daisy had a disaster this week, too?' Hans asked curiously and Megan groaned at the memory.

'The wedding invitations arrived,' she told him. 'I was surprised they'd chosen such a traditional design. They were beautifully printed in a silver script. Unfortunately, they'd spelt Somerby with two Ms.

'It sounds ridiculous, but Daisy was inconsolable — floods of tears. Everyone was against the wedding, she claimed, even the printers. Nothing I said made the slightest difference.'

'There's still plenty of time to get them put right,' Hans pointed out.

'That's what I told her. But no, Daisy reckoned it was an omen.'

'Poor Daisy,' he said, slightly wistfully.

'Yes,' she agreed softly. 'Anyway, she got on the phone to Andy and the tears stopped immediately. I only heard Daisy's side of the conversation, but she was soon laughing. Now, suitably outraged, she's planning to take them back to the shop and demand replacements.'

'Quite right!' Hans was thoughtful for a few moments. 'Andy's very good for Daisy, Megan.'

'Yes, I know.'

He *was* good for her but Megan still wished they would wait instead of rushing headlong into marriage. They wouldn't, she was quite sure of it, but she couldn't stop wishing.

Megan had talked to her own mum about it, several times, but she was no help at all. Quite the reverse in fact. In her day, Mum claimed, any girl not contemplating marriage at nineteen was reckoned to be doomed to spinsterhood. The fact that, at nineteen, Megan had been warned not to get too serious about Richard had been conveniently forgotten . . .

The waiter returned and Megan ordered fruit salad with cream and ice cream. It was delicious — laden with calories. She could never be bothered with counting calories but she was reasonably careful about her diet — until she visited a restaurant. The luxury of having food brought to the table, and leaving the washing up to someone else, always stimulated her appetite.

'Life changes so quickly,' she remarked with a small sigh, when the waiter had left two coffees in front of them. 'In a short time from now, I'll have Flora settled in London and Daisy married. It'll just be me, Joy and a few stray animals.'

140

'And Flora escaping her tyrannical boss whenever the opportunity presents itself,' Hans said with a knowing smile. 'And Daisy and Andy realising that two can only live as cheaply as one when they let someone else keep them for a weekend.'

'I suppose so.' She laughed.

Hans' thoughtful gaze rested on her for a few moments, then he reached into his jacket pocket and brought out a small blue box.

'I'm not saying anything now, Megan,' he told her carefully. 'I know you've got a lot on your mind at the moment and I don't want to rush you. And whether Daisy is making the right decision or not, I don't feel it would be fair to steal her limelight . . .'

He opened the box to give a speechless Megan a brief glimpse of fiery rubies and diamonds.

'But as soon as Daisy is married,' he went on, snapping the box shut, 'I shall come to you, my dear Megan, with gypsy violins, red roses — the lot. I want to pamper you, take care of you and love you for the rest of my days. And,' he warned, blue eyes brimming with warmth, 'although I'm willing to be patient and give you time to think about it, I don't intend to take no for an answer . . .'

The party was just warming up but Mark couldn't stop yawning. He wasn't a great fan of parties at the best of times and, when he'd spent a large portion of the previous night frantically searching for notes, he liked them even less.

Carol, on the other hand, loved them. She and her flatmates would throw them on the flimsiest of excuses. Tonight's was being held simply because they hadn't had one for a while.

The girls' flat was large, but it was also crammed with books, plants, old chairs and strange ornaments. Even with the furniture pushed back against the walls it was cramped. Dozens of candles burned on every surface but, while they gave the rooms a warm glow, they didn't prevent people stumbling into furniture.

Mark glanced at his watch and stifled another yawn. With luck, he would be able to leave in an hour or so.

He wandered into the kitchen and found Carol talking to Brad Bailey. A law student like Carol, Brad had taken the lease of the flat downstairs. Their conversation came to an abrupt halt when Mark appeared and, if he wasn't mistaken, Carol blushed.

'There's plenty of food,' she said in a bright voice. 'Here, Mark — 'She thrust a plate at him. 'Brad? Are you hungry?'

Without waiting for an answer, she piled their plates high with sausage rolls, vol au vents and quiche.

'I'll go and see what's happened to Emma,' she said, striding away from them. 'She's supposed to be sorting out the music . . . '

Left alone, the two men began to eat, without saying anything.

'We were talking about the new Mel Gibson film.' Brad finally broke the silence.

'Oh, right,' Mark answered vaguely. He remembered Carol mentioning it.

'It's being shown this week,' Brad enlightened him. 'Tomorrow's the last night.' He looked at Mark. 'Carol said you couldn't go.'

'No, that's right.' Because Brad seemed to be expecting something else, Mark added, 'I don't know if Carol's going or not.'

'I asked her to come with me. You don't mind, do you?'

'Me? Of course not.'

It was true; he didn't mind. Or he wouldn't have minded, if he hadn't recalled the way their conversation had stopped so abruptly, and the way Carol had blushed. He dismissed the foolish thought.

Word had obviously circulated and the

kitchen door opened, admitting several guests looking for food. Brad wandered off soon afterwards and, soon after that, Mark went in search of Carol — again.

He stayed with her for the rest of the evening, but she didn't mention Brad's invitation until he was leaving. They were downstairs in the communal hall, the first time they'd been alone.

'Brad asked me to go to the cinema with him tomorrow,' she said casually.

'Yes, he told me.' He smiled suddenly. 'He asked me if I minded.'

'And do you?'

'Of course I don't mind. Why should I?'

'No reason, I suppose.' She gave a small sigh.

It was absurd, but he got the feeling that she wanted him to mind. Or perhaps he was imagining things? He hadn't needed a party tonight, he'd needed a good night's sleep.

'It's only the cinema. And it's only Brad. Of course I don't mind.'

'What do you mean?' she demanded. 'Only Brad? What's wrong with Brad? I'll have you know that a lot of girls would be only too pleased for an evening out with him.'

'Yes — but I meant that he was a friend, a neighbour. It's not as if you're going out with a tall, dark stranger who'll whisk you

144

away from me,' he added with a smile. 'Brad presumably wants to see the film and you want to see it. It would be ludicrous to miss it. Besides — ' he laughed softly ' — you'll be able to tell your gran you've been out with Brad and she'll stop dropping hints of wedding bells.'

Carol traced a pattern in the carpet with the toe of her shoe but she didn't comment. She was clearly upset about something and Mark wondered if his remark about her gran had sounded critical. He hadn't meant it to.

'It's no wonder she's having these silly ideas,' he said, trying to make amends. 'Perhaps we see too much of each other, and not enough of other people.'

'Is there someone you want to see more of?'

'No, of course not! But we do spend all our spare time together. Perhaps it's not such a good idea. We don't have any claims on each other, Carol.'

'So we can go out with anyone who takes our fancy?'

'Well — yes, of course.' Something told him it wasn't what she wanted to hear. 'If you want to go out with someone else, you don't need to ask my permission. That's crazy.'

She was making rapid figure-of-eight patterns on the carpet by now.

'We both agreed,' he reminded her, 'that we didn't want to get seriously involved. We've got years of studying ahead of us before we go out into the real world and neither of us can afford any sort of commitment.'

'Right,' she snapped. 'Well, goodnight — '

'Carol!' He was amazed. 'What exactly is the problem here? What do you want me to say?'

'Oh, I think you've said plenty,' she retorted. 'But I wouldn't have been so quick to push you out with someone else.'

'I'm not pushing you,' he argued. 'You're going to the cinema with Brad — that's all. I don't see that it's any big deal.' He remembered that blush again. 'Or is it?' he asked with a frown.

'Apparently not,' she replied furiously. 'And for your information, I told Brad I wouldn't go.' She glared at him. 'But as it doesn't matter to you one way or the other, perhaps I'll tell him I've changed my mind!'

'Carol!'

But she'd gone. She raced up the stairs and then Mark heard the flat door slam shut . . .

'Megan!' Jackie complained.

Megan stopped and turned back to look at her friend. Jackie was several yards behind her, breathing heavily as she struggled to catch up.

'What's your hurry?' Jackie demanded, laughing.

'Sorry. It's such a beautiful day, I could walk for miles.'

'So I noticed. A walk with Rebel, you said. You didn't mention anything about training for a marathon.'

They walked over to the wall and leaned back against it while Rebel explored nearby.

Megan gazed around her, marvelling at how fresh and green the grass and the trees looked. The world was bursting with sturdy growth. The cloudless sky was a deep blue and the sun was warm, even at this early hour.

'What's got into you?' Jackie asked with a curious frown.

'I'm in love.' Megan sighed dreamily.

'So am I! But even in his prime, Tom didn't turn me into an athlete. So how is Hans?'

'Fine.' Megan smiled.

'Fine?' Jackie repeated with a disgusted

grimace. 'He's put an idiotic grin on your face, filled you with boundless energy, made you look disgustingly happy with life — come on, Megan, having been dragged up here at a breakneck pace, I deserve something better than 'fine'. You look like — ' Jackie's eyes widened at the truth of what she was about to say. 'You look like Daisy when she's talking about Andy.'

'Hardly,' Megan protested, but a tell-tale blush coloured her face.

'Hans has asked you to marry him . . . ' Jackie's voice was an awed whisper.

'No! Well, not exactly . . . ' She grinned at her friend's impatient expression. 'He's told me he's going to ask me to marry him,' she explained, adding quickly, 'but not a word to anyone, Jackie. He's waiting until Daisy is married.'

'Megan!' Jackie hugged her, held her at arms length, and hugged her again. 'How could you keep that to yourself?'

'Easily,' Megan insisted on a laugh. 'There's nothing to tell yet. Hans hasn't asked me and I haven't said yes.'

'But you will. Won't you?'

Smiling, Megan nodded. She couldn't quite believe it yet, but yes, she knew exactly what her answer would be — gypsy violins or no gypsy violins. Every few minutes, it hit her afresh. When she woke, it was the first thought that came to mind. It was the last thing on her mind when she fell asleep . . .

'I feel — ' But words failed her.

'If you feel only half as good as you look,' Jackie said with a grin, 'you're feeling terrific.'

'I am,' she agreed happily. 'It's all so unbelievable. When Richard died, I vowed never to look at another man. I never expected to fall in love again and I refused to settle for anything less, just to have a husband and a father for the girls. Then, years later, when I thought that perhaps a little romance would be nice — well, I didn't see anyone worth a second glance.'

Love was the strangest thing, she thought. It would be difficult to imagine two men as different as Richard and Hans. She supposed her love ought to be different, too, but it wasn't. Hans made her feel just as excited, just as wonderful, and just as special as Richard had.

'You would think,' she said slowly, 'that my love for Hans would be a more mature love, wouldn't you?'

'Isn't it?' Jackie asked curiously.

'Not a bit.' Laughing, Megan shook her head. 'I have never felt so reckless, so immature — so happy — in my life.

'It's the simple things that matter, isn't it?' she added thoughtfully. 'It's having someone to share things with — not just problems, but little things that happen during the day.'

Jackie nodded her understanding.

'I'm being boring,' Megan announced apologetically.

'Not in the least.' Jackie laughed. 'What was boring was all that 'Hans is just a friend' and 'my relationship with Hans is purely professional'.' She rolled her eyes. 'Now that *was* boring!'

'Yes, well . . . ' Megan spluttered with laughter.

'Come on,' Jackie said. 'I've got my breath back. Let's walk, and make plans. Where will you be married?'

'We haven't thought,' Megan replied as they set off. 'Hans hasn't officially asked me to marry him yet — remember?'

'But he soon will,' Jackie retorted. 'I'm only surprised he's waiting until Daisy's married. I've never thought of Hans as a patient man. We need to plan, Megan. What will you wear? And where will you live? Hans can't uproot you, can he? What about Joy's schooling . . . ?'

* * *

Colleen welcomed her extended stay in England. She didn't care for the reason behind it, but she loved being able to spend more time with her children . . .

'How's Tony?' Sarah broke into her thoughts.

Colleen took another plate from the rack and dried it.

'He's OK,' she said evasively. 'There are a few problems with the business, but I'm sure he'll work things out. You'll see for yourself tomorrow.

'How's Ben?' she asked, changing the subject.

'As pushy as ever.' Sarah smiled fondly. Her hands were motionless in the bowl of soapy water. 'I like him a lot,' she admitted.

'Is that a problem?' Colleen asked curiously. She'd seen the frown in her daughter's face.

'No,' Sarah answered slowly. She plunged another plate into the water. 'It's just that I wasn't looking for a serious relationship.' She pulled a rueful face. 'But I don't suppose people go looking for these things, do they?' The small frown reappeared. 'And sometimes I think Ben's a bit of a flirt,' she confessed.

Having only met Ben once, Colleen was in no position to judge but she was surprised. She'd spent about fifteen minutes alone with him and she'd gained the impression that he found it difficult to think about anything that wasn't connected with Sarah.

'You mean he flirts with other girls when you're out?'

'Oh, no.' Sarah was quick to deny this. 'No, it's just that I keep thinking of the day we met. One minute he was talking income tax to me, the next he'd charmed a date out of me. It happened so quickly I didn't get chance to think about it.'

'You had long enough to say no,' Colleen pointed out.

'Yes.'

'And that doesn't make him a flirt,' Colleen added. 'If he hadn't acted so quickly, you would have walked out of the office and that would have been that. If you want something, sometimes you have to act quickly, Sarah.'

'But how did he know he wanted to go out with me?' Sarah frowned. 'All he saw was a half pretty face and a girl who was as thick as two short planks when it came to income tax.'

'He saw a *very* pretty face,' she corrected her daughter, laughing. 'Attraction can be instant, Sarah. It can take no time at all to realise that you'd like to get to know someone better.'

'Love at first sight?' Sarah scoffed, hunting

in the bottom of the washing up bowl for any stray spoons.

'I don't know about love,' Colleen answered carefully, 'but attraction at first sight is common enough. If it bothers you, love, talk to him. He seems easy enough to talk to. But I'm sure you don't need to worry. It isn't as if he's asking out every girl who walks into the tax office. He has no free time. He's spending it all with you!'

'I suppose so.' Sarah was finally smiling.

'And it didn't take you long to decide you wanted to go out with him,' Colleen reasoned.

'I liked him as soon as I saw him,' Sarah admitted, 'but I wouldn't have done anything about it. You don't, do you?'

'Ben does. But that makes him brave, not a flirt. You can't condemn him for that, love.'

'You're right.' Sarah was putting plates away but she stopped. 'Thanks, Mum.'

'For what?' Colleen asked quietly. 'I haven't done anything. If you have doubts, you need to talk to Ben.'

'I shall.'

They tidied the kitchen in a companionable silence, then made coffee for four. Colleen carried the tray into the sitting-room and put it down on the table. Jack was strumming away at his guitar, quietly for once, and Ralph was reading a medical paper.

She'd missed all this, Colleen thought sadly, as the four of them chatted.

As soon as they'd finished their coffee, Sarah went to get ready for a date with Ben, and Ralph went to catch up on paperwork in his study.

Colleen watched him go and couldn't help remembering their marriage, and how his disappearances had infuriated her. The days spent with her four young children had been happy, but tiring, and she had longed to relax with Ralph in the evenings. She'd often been disappointed when he vanished to his study.

'If you get up and go,' Jack said with a rueful smile at Colleen, 'I really shall get a complex about my playing.'

'I'm not going anywhere,' she promised with a laugh. She nodded at his guitar. 'Are you hoping to make a living at it?'

'No.' He put his guitar on its stand. 'We've dreamed about being the greatest band in history, of course, but that's all it is, a dream. And I don't imagine it's an easy life, or a very rewarding job.' He grinned suddenly. 'Who said that a job's OK so long as it doesn't degenerate into work?'

'Andy?' Colleen suggested with a chuckle.

'Probably,' Jack agreed.

'So what are you hoping to do, Jack? Are you still thinking about a job in the church?'

'I'm thinking about it.' He nodded then paused for a moment before explaining further. 'I'm not going to follow Dad and Mark into medicine. It's a very worthwhile job — and rewarding — but I'm more interested in caring for souls than bodies. Although I'm not sure I see myself wearing a dog collar, do you? And I'm not sure that I'd be very good at it.'

Colleen thought he would be very good at it. From an early age, his gentle, sensitive nature had softened a very determined spirit. It would be a hard life, though, she couldn't help thinking, and the rewards would be few.

She would have liked to discuss it further but Ben arrived and, predictably, Sarah wasn't ready. Ben wasn't in the least concerned. In his eyes, Sarah could do no wrong. He was a very confident young man, Colleen thought. He was at ease in any company, but he didn't seem over-confident. She liked him.

It was almost ten minutes later before Sarah raced into the room, her red hair flying behind her. They stopped for another few minutes, then left.

'What do you think of Ben?' she asked Jack.

'I think he's great,' he answered immediately. 'Just right for Sarah. It's about time someone taught her to lighten up a little.'

'Lighten up?' she queried with a frown.

'I think she's turning into a glorified housekeeper,' Jack answered. 'Perhaps it's inevitable, being the only female among four males. Perhaps it's our fault for relying on her too much. But she tends to take on the running of the house, making sure everything's where it ought to be, cooking for us . . .'

Like a mother, Colleen thought, and the idea saddened her.

'She seems to enjoy it,' Jack added, 'but I still reckon she needs someone like Ben to show her there's more to life than making sure the freezer's well stocked.'

Dear Jack. Add perception to his many qualities, she thought.

'I like Ben, too,' she said with a smile.

She didn't like the idea of Sarah taking on the role of housekeeper, though . . .

She and Jack chatted until late. Jack went to bed but Colleen sat for a while longer, drinking coffee. It wouldn't help her sleep but she doubted she would sleep anyway.

She was hoping Ralph would join her but she knew from experience that when he got engrossed in something, he lost all track of time.

Finally, she went to his study and tapped lightly on the door.

'It's open,' he called out.

She stepped inside and closed the door behind her.

Ralph rubbed his eyes and looked at his watch.

'Heavens, is that the time? Sorry. I've been neglecting you.'

'I wasn't expecting you to entertain me.' Her smile faded. 'Ralph, are you busy? Can we talk?'

'Of course.' His eyes narrowed. 'Is something wrong?'

She nodded, unsure where to start.

'What is it, Colleen?' he asked curiously.

'It's Tony.' She pulled a chair up by his desk and sat down. 'The business has hit problems.'

'Serious problems?' he asked with surprise.

'Very serious.'

'I'm sorry, I had no idea.'

'Me neither,' Colleen admitted with a sigh. 'I knew something was wrong, of course, but I had no idea it was the business. I'd imagined all sorts of awful things so, at first,

I was relieved to know that it was only the business.'

'And now?' Ralph prompted.

'Now, I'm more worried than ever. Tony's taking it very badly. I keep telling him it's only money — which it is — but he refuses to see it like that. Having started the business from nothing, I suppose it's understandable that he feels his pride's at stake. But I'm worried.'

She rose to her feet and walked over to the window. The curtains hadn't been drawn and she pulled them together, shutting out the darkness, before turning back to face him.

'He's making himself ill, Ralph. He isn't eating or sleeping. The weight's dropping off him. And this week — I'm not sure what happened. Tony said it was just a dizzy spell, but it frightened me. It was three or four minutes before he seemed to know where he was.'

The calm expression on Ralph's face did nothing to reassure her. She knew how good he was at keeping his thoughts hidden.

'It's not the first time it's happened, either,' she went on. 'Tony didn't tell me, but apparently, he had one of these turns earlier in the week. The girl at the hotel asked me how he was, and that was the first I knew of it.'

158

'You've suggested he see his doctor?' Ralph asked.

'Of course! He just accuses me of fussing about nothing.'

'Perhaps you are,' Ralph answered carefully. 'I expect it was nothing more serious than lack of sleep, or lack of food.'

'But what if it is more serious?'

'He should see his doctor. Tony's very sensible,' he went on in what Colleen thought of as his 'don't worry, everything will be all right' voice, 'and I'm sure he'd see his doctor if he thought there was anything to worry about.'

'But I'm not,' she said urgently. 'Ralph — will you talk to him? Please?'

'Me?' Ralph's dark brows shot up. 'And say what? No.' He shook his head. 'I can't talk to him, Colleen. I'm not his doctor — I'm not anything to him. Why should he take note of anything I say? If you can't persuade him to see his doctor, I'm sure I won't be able to.'

'He respects you — '

'Probably because I don't interfere in his life,' Ralph retorted dryly. 'Colleen, if I thought there was anything I could do to help, I would do it. You know I would. But I can't go lecturing Tony on his eating or sleeping habits — Colleen?'

'I'm sorry.' She lifted her face and brushed at her tears.

Ralph stood up and took her shaking hands in his.

'I expect you're worrying about nothing,' he said, his voice gentle with concern.

'Perhaps I am, but — ' She clutched at his hands. 'I can't sit back and watch him head for an early grave.'

She choked back a sob as tears slid down her cheeks.

'I have to do something. I have no right to ask favours, I know, but if you'd just have a word with him. Ralph, please — I don't know where else to turn.'

'Hush . . . ' Ralph put his arms round her and pulled her close. 'I'll talk to him. OK? Tomorrow. I can't promise anything, but I'll talk to him.' He stroked her hair. 'Don't cry, Colleen. Everything will be fine. You'll see.'

Colleen tried to believe him. She tried to convince herself that she was worrying unnecessarily, and that a word from Ralph would solve everything.

She also tried to stop her tears but the unexpected warmth of Ralph's embrace, and the feelings of security it brought, made her cry all the more . . .

7

Flora pushed open the doors to the restaurant and took a moment to catch her breath.

'Sorry I'm late,' she told Hans as she sank into a chair. 'I'd like to blame Doug Nicolson,' she added with a rueful grin, 'but the truth is, I got lost. London takes a bit of getting used to.'

'You're only a few minutes late,' Hans pointed out with amusement.

'I know, but I like to be punctual.' She picked up the menu and studied the tempting dishes on offer. 'I warn you, Hans, I'm starving . . .'

As Hans gave their order to the waiter, it struck Flora that this would be the first proper meal she'd had all week.

Since moving in to her bed-sit last weekend, she had existed on tins and packets of anything that could be warmed up. Her biggest source of nutrition had come from salad sandwiches, eaten at her desk.

'How has your first week been?' Hans asked.

'Hectic, confusing and frustrating on all fronts.' She gave a shrug. 'I've got the bed-sit

161

looking a bit more like home. It's small, of course, but I'm feeling quite cosy. Besides, it's only temporary.'

'And work?'

'Frustrating.' Her mouth tightened. 'I'm sure Doug Nicolson has spent the whole week inventing the most awful jobs for me.'

'I expect he wants to give you time to settle in,' Hans suggested. 'Are you planning to go home for the weekend?'

'No. I'll go next weekend. I'm working tonight. I have to go and see a play with Doug Nicolson. He's been granted an interview with the leading lady and, for some reason which escapes me, I'm expected to tag along. He probably wants me to see the master at work!'

Flora wished she could go home for the weekend. It would be bliss to chat with her mum and Joy, put her feet up and watch television, then climb into her own bed.

But there was no point wishing.

Doug Nicolson had 'suggested' that she might like to go along with him and, as she was very much the new girl, she hadn't felt able to refuse.

The waiter put a plate of food in front of her and Flora breathed in the delicious aroma. A huge Yorkshire pudding was filled with thinly-sliced roast beef and gravy.

Vegetables and roast potatoes circled the pudding.

She put a piece of tender beef in her mouth.

'Oh — delicious. Almost as good as Mum's. Hey, don't forget to tell her you've fed me well,' she added with a chuckle.

'I won't,' Hans promised with amusement.

'How long are you planning to spend in Leicester?' she asked vaguely, her mind on her food.

'Perhaps a week,' he answered.

'As long as that?' She was surprised. 'Any reason? Other than seeing Mum?'

'Isn't that reason enough?'

'Of course.' She laughed. 'Although the neighbours will be buying boxes of confetti.'

He simply smiled and, for a moment, Flora forgot her food. He'd already thought of marriage, she realised. Thought of it and done nothing? That was unlike Hans, the blond tornado she was so fond of.

So what was he waiting for?

'Does it worry you?' he asked suddenly. 'The boxes of confetti, I mean.'

'Me?' She looking into his frowning face. 'Good heavens, no. I'm the least sentimental person I know, but seeing the smile you put on Mum's face can reduce me to tears. You're made for each other, I've been

163

telling Mum that for ages. And she deserves someone. Not to take care of her, she's looked after herself and three kids for years so she's a dab hand at that. But she deserves — well, a bit of romance, I suppose. She should have red roses on Valentine's Day. She should be whisked off for a romantic weekend in Paris at a moment's notice.'

'I'll suggest it,' Hans promised gravely, 'although what Rebel will do if we jet off to Paris for the weekend, I have no idea.'

'You know what I mean.' Flora laughed.

'Yes,' he agreed softly. 'I know what you mean.'

Now, Flora *really* wished she was going home for the weekend . . .

★ ★ ★

Just after four that afternoon, Doug Nicolson stopped by Flora's desk. She was up to her eyes in work and had barely paused for breath all week, but he still managed to make her mentally recap on everything she'd done, just in case there was some crime he could catch her out on.

'Are you still OK for tonight?' he asked.

She could say no, but then he would be able to say she wasn't conscientious.

'Yes.'

'I'll pick you up if you like, then,' he said, adding briskly, 'Seven OK?'

She would have preferred to make her own way there but as it involved either an expensive taxi ride or an extremely complicated tube journey, it seemed ridiculous to refuse.

'Yes. Thanks.'

He nodded and began walking away. Then he paused to call over his shoulder, 'Make sure you're ready. We won't have much spare time.'

Flora refused to give that comment the benefit of a reply. Confound the man! She was never, ever late. Well, except for her lunch date with Hans, but that was different . . .

Just before seven that evening, Flora put on her jacket and stood by the window to watch for Doug Nicolson's car.

She waited, and waited . . .

Finally, at half past seven, his silver coloured car slowed to a stop in front of her house.

'The traffic's murder,' he said as she opened the door and jumped into the passenger seat.

'Really?' Unable to see that his remark qualified as an apology, she fastened her seat belt and made an exaggerated play of checking her watch. 'My watch must be faulty,' she said, all innocence. 'It's strange but I make it half past seven.'

'Sorry.' To her surprise, he laughed. 'I took what should have been a short cut but the road was closed and the diversion was tortuous.' He gave her a sideways glance. 'I'm usually punctual. I hate it when people are late.'

'Me, too,' Flora agreed with an inner smile.

He was right; the traffic was murder. And he wasn't the most patient of drivers.

'Why exactly am I coming along tonight?' she asked.

'I told you, I want a second opinion.' He slowed for the lights. 'I've heard so many different things about Ms Andrews, I'm not sure what to think. And you have a knack of drawing people out of themselves. Added to which,' he continued with a small smile, 'if we're going to slate her performance — '

'Are we?' she interrupted with a frown. 'Surely you haven't made up your mind already?'

'Not at all.' The lights changed to green and he drove off. 'It's almost impossible to open a newspaper or magazine at the moment without seeing her photo, but I

166

gather her acting abilities leave something to be desired.'

'So how come she's getting such plum parts?' Flora asked.

'It's no secret that her father invests a lot of money in her endeavours.'

'But even so, she must be reasonably accomplished. No one's going to put such good parts her way if she's not up to it.'

'One would think not,' he said as he parked the car. 'We'll soon find out. I promised her a big spread so she's given us half an hour after her performance. However, she loves dealing with the media so we might find ourselves joining the queue. If so, we'll leave . . .'

On that uncompromising note, they entered the theatre.

To say Penelope Andrews' performance was bad was an understatement. She was far more interested in presenting her best side to the audience than in the mechanics of the play and her long-suffering prompt deserved a medal.

Afterwards, as they made their way backstage, Flora was still struggling to believe what she'd seen.

'You can do the interview,' Doug announced.

'Me?' Flora's heart gave a panicked leap. She hadn't prepared anything.

167

Before she could argue, however, they found themselves face to face with Penelope Andrews, who, remarkably, looked very pleased with herself.

Much to Flora's surprise, a wealth of questions tumbled out. It was impossible to upset Penelope, she discovered. Even when Flora mentioned the use of the prompt, Penelope just laughed.

'Oh, that. I have a hopeless memory, which is one of the reasons I want to do more TV work. Here, let me get you a drink.'

Flora glanced at Doug. His face was expressionless, but she could see laughter in his eyes.

'What are you planning to write?' he asked as they made their way through the theatre lobby.

'I'm not sure,' she admitted, hating the thought of writing anything bad about Penelope. 'No one could fail to like her, could they? I was expecting someone — well, different. She was born with a solid gold spoon in her mouth. She's beautiful, and spoilt to death. For all that, she's a lovely, warm person. But as an actress — '

Words failed her. She looked at Doug and they both burst out laughing.

Flora's laughter stopped abruptly. Just as they reached the exit, an elderly tramp

168

appeared in front of them, startling her.

'Spare fifty pence for a cup of tea?' the tramp asked hopefully.

Flora's heart was still racing at his sudden, unexpected appearance but Doug calmly reached for his wallet and handed over a note.

'Thank you, sir.' The tramp could hardly believe his good fortune. 'A real gent. A very good evening to you both.'

If the tramp was surprised, Flora was astonished. Only Doug's hand on her arm moved her forwards.

'Where do you buy your cups of tea?' she asked in amazement.

He shrugged.

'It's a case of there but for the grace of God, isn't it? I can afford to be generous. I'm doing the job I enjoy most. I'm my own boss. I have a comfortable home. I eat well.' He turned to look at her. 'Would you like to go for something to eat?'

'Er — yes. Thanks, I'd like that.'

'Good. I know just the place.'

What a night of surprises, Flora thought. And the biggest surprise was discovering that her boss might be human, after all . . .

★ ★ ★

Megan missed having Flora at home. The house seemed so empty all of a sudden, she thought, as she put down her newspaper and wandered into the kitchen.

She'd enjoyed the weekend. Hans made sure there was little time to dwell on how empty the house felt. But during the week it was quiet.

Joy came in and dumped a pile of textbooks on the kitchen table.

'Just look at this lot,' she complained.

Megan automatically put the kettle on.

'Never mind,' she said, 'the summer holidays will soon be here.'

'I suppose so,' Joy said slowly. 'Actually, Mum, I've been thinking . . . '

Megan knew exactly what was coming.

'It's only another year, Joy,' she pointed out. 'You've put in a lot of hard work this year and it would be a shame to give up now. I know you don't think so now, but A-levels are always useful.'

'Not if you want to work with dogs,' Joy argued.

'They could be,' Megan said doubtfully. 'You might want to work with police dogs or join the forces.'

'Train dogs to sniff out bombs or drugs?' She pulled a face. 'Not on your life!'

'Maybe not,' Megan agreed, 'but you'll

have more choice if you have A-levels behind you.'

Joy wasn't convinced. 'I honestly don't see the point of going back to school after the holidays, Mum.'

'But what's the point of giving up now?'

'I could get a job and earn some money,' she said earnestly. 'I'm just wasting my life at school.'

Megan had to sympathise. Her youngest daughter wasn't as bright as Flora and Daisy. Her exam results were just as good but she'd had to work a lot harder. Megan could see her point, too. There were few subjects on the school curriculum of interest to a girl who had her heart set on training dogs.

'Why not talk it over with Flora or Daisy?' she suggested.

Before Joy could argue, the doorbell rang. 'I'll get it,' she said.

Megan heard Andy's voice and went into the hall to see if Daisy was with him. She wasn't.

'Andy! What a surprise. Come in. Is Daisy all right?'

'Fine,' he replied. 'I've got a couple of days off so I decided to come home for the day. I'm on my way back to Manchester now.'

'We've just made a pot of tea,' Megan told him as they walked to the kitchen.

'I timed that right,' he said with a grin. 'I really came to give you this.' He handed over the parcel that had been clutched under his arm.

While Joy poured another cup of tea, Megan opened the parcel. She'd guessed it was one of his photographs but she hadn't expected it to have such an effect on her. In a plain frame, set in an oval mount, was a photo of Daisy.

'Andy, it's beautiful.'

'She's a beautiful subject,' he said fondly, 'but yes, I'm pleased with it.'

Megan gazed at the photo of her daughter. Daisy was smiling, an almost secret smile, but the love for the man behind the camera was clear for all to see. She was radiant with happiness.

No matter what happened in the future, Megan thought, they would always have this photo showing Daisy at her happiest.

'Thanks, Andy,' Megan said, touched by the gesture. 'I'll treasure it always.'

Over a cup of tea, Joy complained to Andy about her schoolwork and Andy told them about his job at the lab which was going well. He had also been commissioned to take the publicity photos for a new hotel and conference centre.

Megan's feelings for Andy changed every time she saw him.

At first, she'd thought him irresponsible, but she supposed that was only because she knew he was just back from Australia and New Zealand on a back-packing trip, and because he'd asked Daisy to marry him after such a short time.

Now, all Megan saw was a young man who was more than capable of taking care of her daughter. He was willing to accept responsibility, and he was well aware of the struggle that lay ahead if he was to make a name for himself as a photographer.

He didn't stay long, he was too eager to get back to Daisy, and he offered Joy a lift to her friend's house. As Megan waved goodbye from her front door, she felt like she was finally getting to know her future son-in-law.

Some time later, Hans arrived.

With his usual exuberance, he lifted Megan off her feet and swung her round. Anyone would think they hadn't seen each other for months.

'Do I have you all to myself?' he asked.

'For the time being.'

Hans spotted the photograph of Daisy and picked it up.

'Andy's work?' he guessed.

'I doubt if Daisy could look like that for any other photographer,' Megan answered with wry amusement.

'She looks just like you,' he murmured.

'She looks very young,' Megan corrected him, 'and very much in love.'

Laughing, Hans returned the photo to its spot.

'As I said, she looks just like you.' He clasped her hands in his. 'You look very young, and, although I don't know about *very much* in love, I'm sure I see a certain — '

'I am in love,' she broke in softly. 'Very much in love. I don't need time to think, Hans, and I certainly don't need red roses or gypsy violins. All I need is you. I love you and I want to marry you . . . '

★ ★ ★

June had turned into a stiflingly hot month and Ralph had thought he might be roasted alive on the short drive from the surgery to his house. He got out of the car and saw that despite Sarah's constant ministrations with the watering can, the young plants in the tubs by the front door were wilting.

He went inside and headed for the kitchen.

'Hi, Dad. You just missed Mark.' Sarah looked up from the fabric she was working on. 'He rang to say he couldn't make it on Friday so he's driving back on Saturday instead.'

Ralph took off his tie and unfastened his shirt collar.

'How is he?'

'Like a bear with a sore head.' Sarah rolled her eyes expressively. 'It's no wonder Carol dumped him.'

'Did she? Dump him?' It was news to Ralph, although he had noticed that his eldest son had been a little quiet on his last visit.

'As good as. Mark suggested they see less of each other — you know how stuffy and serious he can be — and I gather Carol took offence. They haven't spoken since. Oh, and Penny called in this afternoon. Did she tell you?'

'I haven't seen her.' He poured himself a glass of chilled orange juice. 'What did she want?'

'Me.' Sarah grinned at him. 'She wants me to make her a quilt. I said I'd have a think, then give you some designs to take in to her tomorrow. Mind you,' she added with a frown, 'I'm up to my eyes in work at the moment. I haven't even started on Andy and Daisy's yet and the wedding's in three weeks.'

'Don't remind me.' Ralph groaned.

'We'll have a house full of people. I honestly didn't think Aunt Beatrice would travel, did you?'

'No, but she's never been the type to sit back and age gracefully.' Ralph grinned suddenly. 'We'd better lock the sherry away.'

Sarah spluttered with laughter and, as they drank their tea, they reminisced about family weddings and christenings . . .

Jack came in for his meal, then left again to practice with the band.

Ralph had treated himself to a new CD and, as only Sarah was home, he thought he might be able to listen to it in peace. Even over the headphones, however, he was aware of Sarah's heavy sighs. She was sitting on the sofa, drawing in her sketch pad. Finally, Ralph gave up. He removed his headphones and switched off the CD.

'Something wrong?' he asked, and she looked up, surprised.

'Sorry, was I disturbing you? No — I just want to come up with something special for Penny's quilt. Something that suits her personality.'

Ralph wished he could help but designing a quilt to suit someone's personality stretched his imagination beyond its limits.

'What do you think?' she asked.

'Me? I've no idea.'

'You must have,' she retorted. 'How long have you known her?'

'It's twelve years since she joined the practice.'

'There you are then. If you don't know her, no one does. I suppose,' Sarah said thoughtfully, 'she's an ice and fire type of person, isn't she? You know — a cool, composed and practical exterior hiding a very passionate nature.'

Ignoring her dad's bemused expression, she went on, 'And she's a lot like you, I suppose. It would be difficult to find two people who had more in common.'

They'd had this conversation before and Ralph refused to have it again.

'We're both GPs and we're both divorced,' he pointed out dryly.

'There are none so blind,' she murmured, before losing herself once more in her sketches.

Ralph didn't know what to make of that remark but he knew better than to ask questions . . .

The following morning, when the last of the patients had gone, he carried several sketches into Penny's surgery.

'These are just to give you an idea, I gather,' he told her. 'Sarah says she's happy to work on your own ideas, or come up with something else.'

'These are lovely.' Penny spread the coloured sketches across her desk. 'Your daughter's very talented, Ralph.'

'She is,' he agreed with a touch of pride.

There was a varied selection of designs, Ralph noticed. A few had a traditional feel, which he guessed Penny would prefer, but most were modern.

'Oh, this one's perfect,' Penny exclaimed suddenly. 'I love the reds and oranges with the blues and whites.' She carried the sketch to the window to examine it more closely.

'Ice and fire,' she murmured, reading Sarah's pencil notes on the back of the sketch.

'Ice and — ?' Ralph frowned. 'Really?'

'That's what she calls it.' Penny nodded. 'I love it. Don't you, Ralph?'

'It was designed to suit your personality,' he said vaguely.

Ralph had known Penny for twelve years, but he had never thought of her as anything other than an exceptionally good doctor and a valued colleague. What had Sarah said? There are none so blind . . .

Since Penny's divorce, five years ago,

Ralph had taken her out to lunch or dinner many times, and they'd shared problems, both personal and professional, but Ralph couldn't say in all honesty that he really knew Penny. In fact, it seemed his daughter knew her better.

'My personality?' Penny broke into his thoughts.

'She sees you as ice and fire,' he explained. 'She thinks you have a cool, composed exterior hiding a passionate nature.'

Penny didn't laugh, as he'd expected. She considered his words for a moment.

'I suppose that goes with the job,' she said at last. 'We show the world a quietly calm unflappable front while, underneath, we can be raging about the lack of facilities, panicking we've missed some vital symptom, worrying what any tests will show. Our real selves, passionate or otherwise, have to be constrained.'

She laughed suddenly.

'Mind you, apart from being very talented and having a highly fertile imagination, your daughter is also an incurable romantic. She'll see me as the person she wants me to be. And I think she wants me to be a deeply passionate person who'll sweep you off your feet, Ralph.'

'Probably.' Ralph laughed.

'Not that I'm against being wined and dined in style. You owe me dinner, Ralph. If you remember, the last time we arranged to go out, Colleen turned up. How is she, by the way? Still in London?'

'Yes. I assume she'll stay until the wedding now.'

'Sarah was talking about the wedding plans yesterday,' she said. 'It must be strange for you and Colleen, discussing Andy's marriage. You live separate lives, but the children tie you together for life, don't they?'

He nodded.

'There's no such thing as a clean break when children are involved.'

Penny gazed at him for long moments.

'Ralph, do you still love Colleen?'

The question shook him. No one had ever asked him that before.

In his experience, people assumed that at the precise moment the divorce was signed and sealed, both parties automatically stopped loving each other. And he knew that didn't happen.

Penny deserved an honest answer, but Ralph was no longer sure what the truth was . . .

★ ★ ★

180

Colleen was surprised by the number of people in Hyde Park at such an early hour. A lot of people listened to personal stereos as they jogged their way to fitness. Some strode out purposefully, as if the park were just a convenient short cut. Others took time to enjoy the perfect morning.

Colleen walked slowly, hoping the clear blue sky and sunshine would colour her mood, but it didn't seem to be working.

She glanced at her watch. It was time she retraced her steps.

Tony had been sleeping when she left and she'd scribbled a note for him so he wouldn't worry when he woke.

She wondered if he'd even notice . . .

For weeks now, he'd seemed incapable of thinking of anything other than the business. It meant a lot to him, more than she'd realised perhaps, and she knew he was under immense pressure to save it and the jobs of those back home.

All the same, she couldn't help feeling that, as far as Tony was concerned, she might as well not exist.

He hadn't spoken about the business for days, and Colleen hadn't asked. In fact, they barely spoke at all these days.

She didn't need to be told that things were going badly; his constant black moods told her all she needed to know. And if everything had turned out as Tony had hoped, they would have been back home in California weeks ago.

She would have liked nothing better than to offer help and support, but it was difficult to do that when Tony was so determined to shoulder everything alone and shut her out . . .

Her spirits sank even lower as she walked into the hotel, ignored the lift and walked slowly up the stairs to their room.

Tony was sitting by the window, an unopened newspaper in his hand. He turned and frowned at her.

'I wish you wouldn't go wandering around on your own, Colleen.'

'I needed some fresh air and exercise,' she replied lightly as she kissed him. 'Are you ready for breakfast? I'm starving.'

'Yes, why not?'

The dining-room was crowded and Colleen was conscious of the silence at their table. Laughter sounded around other tables as plans were made.

Tony's breakfast consisted of one slice of toast, which Colleen suspected was only eaten because she was there, and two cups of strong, black coffee.

'I've booked us on Friday's flight,' he

announced suddenly.

Colleen stared at him, aghast, but it was impossible to know what he was thinking.

'Friday?' she repeated incredulously. 'But — why?'

'Because there's nothing left here for me,' he said flatly. 'I need to get home and instruct the lawyers to start winding things up.'

'Oh, Tony.' Her heart went out to him. Despite the level tone of voice, she knew just how it hurt him to talk about it. 'Is there nothing else we can do?'

'Nothing.' He nodded at her empty coffee cup. 'Have you finished?'

'Yes.'

He stood up and waited for her to do likewise.

That was it, end of conversation, Colleen realised, as they walked up the stairs to their room.

Tony closed the door behind them and Colleen stood in the centre of the room with her arms folded.

'Is that how much I matter to you, Tony?' she asked shakily. 'You tell me we're flying home on Friday, you tell me the business is finished — is that it?'

'What else is there to say?' Impatience flashed across his face.

183

'I'd say there was plenty,' she retorted. 'This is one of the most important things we've ever faced.'

'It's *the* most important but that doesn't mean — '

'No,' she argued. 'The most important things concern our life together, the children, our marriage.'

'And talking about every single thing that brought the company to its knees won't help. The advertising industry has always been fickle, you know that.' He spoke patiently which, of late, meant that his patience was rapidly running out. 'I made a mistake taking on Vic Douglas and now we're paying for it. There's nothing else to say on the subject.'

'So what happens now?' she pressed.

'We go home and I tell a lot of people that they no longer have a job. Then I decide how we're supposed to live in the future . . . '

'You decide? Why you, Tony? Don't I have any say in the matter?'

'I meant *we* decide.' He brushed past her. 'I don't want to discuss it, Colleen. Not now.'

He stood at the window with his back to her.

Colleen could see the defeat in his shoulders. She longed to reach out to him, but she knew he would reject her.

184

'I can't go back on Friday,' she said calmly.

'What do you mean?' He spun round to frown at her.

'It's Andy's wedding in two weeks.'

'We'll come back for that.' He was still frowning.

'But I want to be here. Everything's under control, I know, but I still want to be here. I'm his mother, Tony, I should be here.'

'I see. And where will you stay?' His voice was like ice.

'Here. Or in Leicester.' He hadn't given her time to think. 'I don't know, Tony.'

'So you'll go running to Ralph? Well, there's nothing new there, is there. That's exactly what you've always done.'

'What's that supposed to mean?' she cried in astonishment.

'All the time we've been married — the slightest thing and you've been straight on the phone to Ralph. Good old Ralph. You even got him to nag me about having a check up with my doctor . . . '

'I was worried about you. I still am!'

'My point exactly. Who do you turn to when you're worried? Who have you always turned to when you're worried? Ralph!'

'You're being ridiculous.' Colleen refused to be drawn into an argument. 'Of course

I want to be here. Andy's getting married. Mark will be his best man. Sarah's to be a bridesmaid and Jack's supplying the music afterwards. It's a big event in my children's lives and, just for once, I want to share it with them.

'In any case, there's nothing I can do to help you, is there? You won't let me help. You never have, Tony!'

'Just being there would help,' he snapped.

Colleen walked over to him and put her hand on his arm, but he brushed it aside.

'Go and stay with Ralph. I'll fly over for the wedding and tell you exactly what we have left. I'll let you know if we still have a roof over our heads. Then it will be up to you, Colleen. You'll have to decide on which side of the Atlantic your future lies . . .'

8

Megan gazed across the sea of wedding guests to where her daughter was dancing with her new husband.

The day had passed happily, and Daisy had looked radiant — as every bride should. Andy had seemed confident, and he'd been bursting with happiness as he put his ring on his bride's finger.

The bridesmaids, Flora, Joy and Sarah had looked spectacular in their long, blue dresses. They'd carried small baskets of flowers and even Joy had managed to look poised and elegant.

The speeches had been short, and fairly jovial, but touching nonetheless. Ralph had welcomed Daisy to his family with a sincerity that had moved Megan. Mark, speaking as Andy's best man, had been equally welcoming.

Megan's thoughts had been on Richard often during the day. He would have been proud of his daughters. Just as she was.

But it was time to move on. Daisy was married. Flora had settled in London so well people would think she'd been born there.

187

Even Joy, the baby of the family, would soon be making her own way in the world.

The changes made Megan a little wistful, but she refused to be anything but optimistic . . .

'It makes you feel old, doesn't it?' Colleen's voice broke into her thoughts.

'A little.' Megan turned to smile at her. 'But I'm not as worried as I was when they first told me they were getting married. They seem terribly young, but I think — hope — they'll have a good marriage.'

'Andy's far more serious than people think, you know,' Colleen said softly. 'Although Jack — ' She rolled her eyes. 'I'll apologise now for the music. I told him it would be far too loud.' She gazed across the hotel's lounge to where her youngest son was playing his guitar. 'I'm convinced he'll end up as a vicar, but looking at him now — what a thought that is!'

They both laughed.

'Have you decided when you're going back to California?' Megan asked.

'Monday.'

'Oh, no!' Megan had known Tony was in a rush to get back, but she hadn't imagined they would be leaving quite so soon. 'I was hoping we could get together.'

'That would have been nice.' Colleen

spoke with regret. 'But Tony's so tied up with the business, and he needs to be there.' She gave Megan a bright smile. 'We must keep in touch.'

'We must,' she agreed. 'I'll let you know how Andy and Daisy are getting on. I know Ralph will, too, but — '

'I know.' Smiling, Colleen put her hand on Megan's arm. 'Men don't notice things quite the same. I was hoping the Californian sun might tempt Andy and Daisy for their honeymoon,' she admitted. 'But there, who'd want to spend their honeymoon with their mother — mother-in-law?' She pulled a face and grinned. 'I don't feel like a mother-in-law.'

'I know just what you mean . . . And I'm sure they would have loved California. They're only going to Scotland because Andy's getting paid to take some photos. I think it's very responsible of them.'

'So do I,' Colleen answered with a laugh. 'I just wish someone was paying him to take photos in California. Not that they'll care where they are,' she added fondly.

'Sarah will miss you,' Megan said softly.

'Oh, don't. In all these years — and it makes no difference that they're all old enough to take care of themselves — I have never grown used to leaving them. I always spend the flight fighting back tears.'

'Come on,' Megan said lightly, 'we can't be gloomy today. Let's grab another glass of champagne and see if we can find someone to dance with us. Good heavens, look!' She pointed to where Mark and Flora had taken over the dance floor and were doing an energetic dance demonstration — rock and roll style.

'I think I'll wait for a nice slow waltz.' Colleen laughed.

'Me, too . . .'

Later, Megan noticed Ralph standing on the edge of the room, watching Colleen as she spoke to Mark. Ralph spent a lot of time watching Colleen, and Megan couldn't help wondering how he felt. There was nothing to be learned from his expression, but his eyes rarely strayed from his ex-wife . . .

'I shall miss Colleen,' she told Hans. 'We've become good friends. The last-minute wedding panic would have worn me down, but she made it fun.'

'I'm sure she'll soon be back for a visit,' he said. 'In any case, you won't have time to miss her. You'll be too busy planning your own wedding.'

'Yes.' She looked up and smiled at him. 'And I know who won't be asked to play the music — I swear we shall all be deaf by morning. We'll have a party, shall we, and announce it then? When Daisy and Andy are back from their honeymoon?'

'Anything you like.'

'A big party and a small wedding? Just the family?'

'Whatever you say,' he murmured, and Megan laughed.

'A great help you are!'

Across the room, Colleen was watching Megan and Hans. She was surprised, and annoyed with herself, for feeling a touch of envy. There was nothing forced about Hans' smile as he spoke to Megan. There was nothing forced about the answering light in Megan's eyes . . .

'You're looking very thoughtful,' Ralph said, and she turned to smile at him.

'I was thinking that Mark grows more like you every day.' It was a thought she'd had many times during the day.

'And Sarah grows more like you.' He put out his arm. 'Dance?'

She searched the room, spotted Tony talking to Andy and nodded.

'Yes — while they're playing something that *can* be danced to.'

'Bedlam, isn't it?' Ralph laughed. 'Still, it's probably no worse than the racket we

191

had at our wedding. We're just less able to appreciate it.'

They made their way onto the dance floor.

'Andy's chosen well, don't you think, Ralph?'

'Daisy's a lovely girl,' he answered, and Colleen gave him a sharp look.

'You still have reservations? After seeing them today? You couldn't wish for a happier couple.'

'I know, but there's a world of difference between a wedding and struggling to ends meet at such a young age. I only hope they're as happy in five years.'

'They will be.' Colleen felt certain of it.

'Sarah will miss you when you go back,' he said, changing the subject.

'You're the second person who's said that.' She sighed. 'I shall miss her — dreadfully.'

'We'll all miss you,' he said softly.

'You'll be glad to get back to normal,' she teased him. 'All I've done is burden you with my worries.'

'No . . . I shall miss you. We all will . . . How's Tony?' he asked. 'I mean, really. I did ask him, but got my head bitten off.'

'Sorry — he's under a lot of pressure.' Her spirits had sunk when she'd met him at the airport — he looked worse than he had when he'd left London. 'He's OK, I suppose. Or he will be, when the lawyers can start sorting things out with the business . . . '

When the dance ended, Colleen went to find Tony and coaxed him onto the dance floor.

He danced well, but she knew he was simply going through the motions. His mind was miles away.

'Do we have to go home on Monday?' she asked quietly. She felt sure a holiday would do him good. 'Can't we stay another week? We could head off to the country and relax — just the two of us?'

'You can stay, if that's what you want.' His look was guarded. 'I have to get back, you know I do.'

She knew it, but she longed to stay. Mark would be busy with his studies, Andy would be on his honeymoon and adjusting to married life, and Jack would be on a walking holiday with a few pals. Only Sarah would be at home — but it was Sarah that Colleen longed to spend time with. Just when she was getting closer to her daughter, she would be putting that great ocean between them again.

'Will you stay?' he asked, as she hadn't answered.

'Of course not.' She gave him a bright

smile. 'I want to be with you.'

She glanced across the room and caught Ralph watching her. She couldn't fathom the expression on his face, but it caused a shiver to run through her veins . . .

★ ★ ★

Soon after Daisy and Andy left for their honeymoon, life seemed to return to normal for the Somerbys and the Pettifers.

Flora threw herself wholeheartedly into her work. She was incredibly busy, but loved every minute of it.

One morning, she marched into Doug Nicolson's office, ready to defend her choice of pictures to accompany an article, and felt sure he'd disagree with her. But the sight of him sent all arguments from her mind. He was sitting at his desk, with the phone in his hand, and a very thoughtful expression on his face.

He looked up as she entered and, very slowly, replaced the receiver.

'Problems?' Flora asked curiously.

'No,' he answered slowly. 'I was just speaking to Hans. He invited me to a party — tonight.'

'Oh, right. Yes, Mum's throwing a party,' she told him. 'It's a sort of 'welcome back from honeymoon' party for Daisy and Andy.'

She stopped short as the implication hit her. 'Just the family', Mum had said. So why had Hans invited Doug? She slapped her hand to her forehead.

'Just the family, my foot! I thought she sounded strange. It's not a party for Daisy and Andy at all — well, it might be, but it's more than that. I remember seeing Hans smile — they're getting married!'

'What?' He laughed at her earnest expression. 'You can't possibly know that!'

'I can.' She dropped the transparencies on his desk. 'I need to dash out and buy a present.'

'Would you like a lift to Leicester?'

She paused, her hand on the door.

'What time are you leaving?'

'I can get you there before the train would,' he said with a smile, and she laughed.

'Yes, please . . . '

Later that afternoon, Flora could hardly contain her excitement as Doug drove them towards Leicester.

'There is a possibility you're wrong,' he pointed out.

'I don't think so. What exactly did Hans say?' she asked, and he groaned with amusement.

'You've asked me a dozen times, Flora. I

told you — he didn't say anything out of the ordinary. All the same, I did get the impression that he had more on his mind than business.'

'There you are then!'

'Conclusive proof,' he agreed with a wry smile as he stopped the car outside the house.

Doug didn't stop the engine and Flora looked at him in surprise.

'Aren't you coming in?'

'No, this is family time.' He seemed equally surprised by the question. 'I'll see you later — at the hotel.'

'Hotel?'

'Yes, at the — ' Now he did switch the engine off. 'When Hans told me where the party was being held, I booked a room at the same hotel.' He frowned suddenly. 'Where did you think it was being held?'

'Here. At home.' Her eyes danced with laughter. 'Our family's not so big that we need to book hotels. Oh, really! Aren't they hopeless at surprises?'

'Flora — '

'I know,' she cut him off, 'I could be wrong.' But she knew she wasn't. 'Thanks for the lift, Doug. I'll see you later. And remember to be suitably surprised . . . '

'You've just missed Daisy and Andy,'

196

Megan told Flora as she greeted her at the door. 'They're at Andy's dad's. They'll be back soon. And Hans is — he'll be here soon.

'Was that Doug who brought you home?' she asked, changing the subject. 'Why didn't you bring him in?'

'It's the strangest thing,' Flora answered innocently, 'but he seems to think this party's being held at a hotel.'

'Oh, right.' Megan flushed. 'We thought we'd invite some friends, as well as the family. Hans has invited quite a few. Anyway, I'm pleased Doug could come, I'm looking forward to meeting him. How are you getting on with him these days?'

'Fine,' Flora answered slowly. 'He's not the easiest of people to work for, or with, but he has his good points.' She grinned. 'He likes to keep them well hidden, but they're there. Yes, I can understand why he and Hans are friends.'

What she couldn't understand was the attraction he held for her. She couldn't deny it, but neither could she understand it. She remembered the evening they saw the play, when Doug gave money to the old tramp. She remembered having a meal with him afterwards. It was difficult to equate him with the man who could snap at his staff

197

for no good reason at all. He was extremely lucky that every last one of them managed to take his comments with a good-natured shrug. She'd had lunch with him, and dinner last Friday night. Both occasions had been more business than personal, but — .

She dismissed her thoughts. She couldn't make sense of them, so there was no point thinking them. Doug was her boss and she was still the new girl. She refused to acknowledge any other feelings . . .

They caught up on news, and it was an hour later when Flora took her case upstairs. She was about to throw herself down on her own comfortable bed, and she scowled at the big hairy lump lying there.

'Joy! What's this animal doing on my bed?' Rebel stretched and slowly, very slowly, climbed off the bed.

Joy put her head round the door.

'He likes your bed best,' she explained sheepishly. 'We keep shutting the door, but he keeps opening it.'

With a shake, and another stretch, Rebel walked past them and out of the room.

Flora brushed a disgusted hand across her quilt, then sat on her bed.

'What's going on?'

'What do you mean?' Joy sat beside her.

'Mum. This party. What's it in aid of?'

'Daisy and Andy are going back to Manchester on Monday so Mum thought it would be nice to have a party. Andy has to get back to work.'

'So why book a hotel?' Flora scoffed. 'No, there's more to it than that. I think it's an engagement party.'

Joy stared back at her, not understanding.

'Mum and Hans!' Flora announced.

The sound of footsteps racing up the stairs ended the conversation. Daisy ran into the room and hugged Flora.

'Tell me everything,' Flora said, patting the bed beside her. 'What was the weather like? What did you do? Was it wonderfully romantic?'

'Romantic?' Daisy spluttered with laughter. 'I spent the entire time protecting whichever camera Andy wasn't using from the rain. It rained every day. But the hotel was wonderful. Old-fashioned and cosy. It was supposed to be haunted, too. We had a four-poster bed. The trouble was, Andy was up at the crack of dawn to catch the best light.' She sighed happily. 'It was perfect. Just perfect.'

Flora smiled, and hoped that Daisy would be equally happy when she realised the honeymoon was over . . .

'Flora reckons Mum and Hans are getting

engaged,' Joy said with a frown.

'What?' Daisy gasped. 'Oh, Flora — I hadn't thought of that. I knew there was something going on. She's been behaving strangely since we got back.'

'As soon as I heard Hans had invited Doug — ' Flora looked at her sisters. 'I hope I'm right.'

'So do I,' Joy said fervently.

'Me, too,' Daisy said. 'I'll have to tell Andy to take his camera and get some good pictures of — ' Her voice stopped as their mother came into the room.

'This party tonight — ' Megan sought the right words. 'Hans and I thought — we were planning to surprise you, but sometimes surprises can be horrible, can't they?'

The sisters exchanged bemused glances as Megan sat next to Joy on the crowded bed.

'The thing is,' Megan went on, colouring slightly, 'Hans and I are going to — ' she took a huge breath — 'Hans has asked me to marry him, and I've said yes. We planned to announce it tonight, but then I started to worry that it might come as a bit of a shock — Flora?' Her voice rose. 'What's so funny?'

'You are!' Despite her laughter, tears pricked Flora's eyes as she hugged her mum. 'I'd guessed, but I'm so happy for

200

you. It's high time you made an honest man of the blond tornado . . . '

★ ★ ★

The party was a great success. Flora didn't think she'd ever seen her mum look happier. Her glance kept dropping to her finger, where Hans' ring sparkled beneath the lights.

The wedding was to be a simple affair, they'd said, in three weeks, with just the immediate families present. Flora would have expected Hans to want something on a grander scale, but he seemed willing to go along with anything Megan wanted.

She looked around the room and saw that Doug was still talking to her gran. He'd been there for almost an hour, since Hans had introduced them.

Flora was about to go and rescue him when she saw him say something, look at his watch, and walk away. It looked as if he was leaving.

She ran to catch him up.

'You're not leaving, are you?'

'Of course not. I was going downstairs to get some coffee,' he said. 'Want some?'

'Good idea.' They walked along the corridor to the lift. 'Sorry about gran.'

'Don't be,' he replied with amusement.

'She's a fascinating woman. She was telling me about that magazine you used to edit,' he went on with a laugh. 'Ballet Weekly, wasn't it?'

'Don't!' Flora cringed at the memory. She'd been about eight years old at the time, and the 'magazine' had been circulated to any of her friends who shared her passion for ballet dancing.

'Are you enjoying yourself?' she asked, changing the subject.

'Of course.' The answer was automatic and Flora smiled.

'You're not a party person, are you?'

'Does it show?' He grimaced. 'I must admit that I usually avoid them. This time, however, Hans caught me unawares.' He gave her a sideways smile. 'I suppose you're feeling very smug. I'm surprised — I had Hans tagged as a confirmed bachelor.'

'No!' Flora scoffed.

'He's avoided matrimony for a good few years,' Doug pointed out dryly.

'Well, yes — but sometimes it takes a while for the right person to come along.'

'Apparently.'

They stepped into the lift.

'That piece you did on Penelope Andrews,' Doug said. 'It was good — I liked it.'

As he hadn't commented at the time, Flora

had assumed he'd thought it acceptable. The praise came as a welcome surprise, though.

'I was thinking about the Christmas issue,' he went on. 'I think — '

Suddenly, Flora let out a startled cry as it jerked to a stop, and they were plunged into darkness. She instinctively grabbed Doug's arms.

As suddenly as the lights had gone out, they came back on and the lift carried on as if nothing had happened.

'A power failure I expect,' Doug murmured. 'It probably took a moment for the generator to kick in.'

Flora nodded and laughed shakily at her own panic.

When they reached the ground, the lift doors slid open. Neither moved. Flora's hands were still on Doug's arms and she was reluctant to move them. She gazed into his face as the lift doors silently closed again.

His kiss was everything Flora had imagined. Despite trying to keep such thoughts from her mind, she'd spent a lot of time imagining how it would feel to be held in his arms and kissed. And it felt wonderful — and right.

She could feel his heart beating just as quickly as her own. His arms were tight around her as his mouth moved over hers.

Her soft sigh, a sigh of pleasure, broke the spell. Her lips were left aching for his and she felt his hands drop to her waist. She opened her eyes, missing his warmth.

His expression was grim as he pushed her back from him.

'We'll put that down to the champagne,' he said as he reached for the button to open the doors. 'I don't suppose you're used to it.'

'What?' She felt as if he'd slapped her in the face. 'I only had half a glass!'

'Then we'll put it down to the champagne *I* had,' he replied grimly, managing to hit the button this time.

The doors opened and his hand went beneath her elbow, urging her out of the lift.

'Do we have to put it down to anything?' She stopped to look at him. 'It's not the first time I've been kissed, and I'm sure it isn't the first time you've been kissed.'

'Flora, I don't believe mixing business with pleasure.' He spoke with exaggerated patience. 'It never works. I could give you a hundred examples — it's a recipe for disaster.'

'I didn't realise we were,' she retorted, stung by his words. 'I thought that was pleasure. Or are you saying — '

'I'm saying it won't happen again.' His expression betrayed none of his feelings. 'Now, if you'll excuse me.'

Flora watched him stride away. She wasn't sure if she wanted to throw something heavy at his retreating back, or throw herself down on the carpet and burst into tears . . .

★ ★ ★

On the following Tuesday afternoon, Sarah poured out two cups of coffee and put one in front of Penny.

'I really shouldn't be here. I've got a million things to do at the surgery.'

'What's a few more minutes?' Sarah sat opposite her and held a few swatches together to compare the results. They were choosing material for a quilt that was to be a present for Penny's as yet unborn great-niece or nephew. 'So what do you think? Shall we go for bright reds and yellows? Blue and pink are out of the question until we know if it's a boy or a girl.' She looked up. 'Does she know what it's going to be?'

'No.' Penny smiled. 'She keeps saying she doesn't mind, but she's got three girls and I know she's desperate for a boy.' She shook her head with amusement. 'I'm glad she's your dad's patient, not mine. She's read so many books on the subject, she probably knows more than Ralph.'

Penny turned over a couple of sketches. 'This is my favourite. And yes, the reds and yellows. It will be lovely and cheerful.'

'Right.' Sarah scribbled a few notes. 'Let me know as soon as it's born and I'll get the date of birth put on it.'

'Oh, lovely.'

'It makes it more personal,' Sarah agreed. 'If they decide on a name, we'll get that put on it, too.' She checked her watch. 'I was expecting Dad home by now.'

'He had a lot of calls to make this afternoon. A GP's lot is not an easy one.' Penny sighed dramatically.

'Hey, why not stay for — '

'Because I have to get back to the surgery. And because I've already made plans for this evening.' Penny smiled at her. 'It's kind of you to offer, but I really can't.'

'Tomorrow?' Sarah suggested.

'No.' Penny took a sip of coffee. 'Sarah — I'm flattered, I really am, but your dad and me — it's not going to happen.'

'I was only suggesting you stay for dinner.' But Sarah's blush said more than her words did.

'No, you weren't. You were hoping — well, I'm not sure what you hope for, but it isn't going to happen. I think the world of your dad, you know that. He's a good doctor, a good colleague, and probably too attractive for his own good,' she added with a smile. 'We work well together, Sarah, but that's all we ever will do. I'm happy as I am. I'm sure Ralph is, too.'

'Don't you get lonely?' Sarah ventured.

'No. I'm too busy.' Her voice grew more gentle. 'I'm sure your dad doesn't, either. He has his work, he has you children, and he has plenty of friends.' She finished her coffee and rose to her feet. 'I really must go, Sarah. Thanks for coffee. And there's no immediate rush for the quilt.'

Sarah showed her out, then returned to the table to tidy away the fabric. Penny could say what she liked, but Sarah reckoned her dad *did* get lonely. Lately, she'd caught him more than once with a faraway look in his eyes.

He and Penny would be perfect for each other, too. It wasn't just work — they got along well on a personal level.

The phone rang and she went to pick it up.

'Sarah?'

'Mum!' Sarah pulled up a chair, ready for a chat. 'You OK?'

'No — not really.' Colleen's voice was tight. 'Is your dad there?'

'No, but he shouldn't be long. Do you want him?'

'Yes — no.' There was a long pause. 'I thought I'd better let you know — I'm at the hospital. Tony's had a heart attack.'

'Oh, Mum, no!' The level tone of Colleen's voice frightened her. 'But he'll be all right, won't he?'

'I don't know, love. They say it's too soon to tell. Anyway,' she went on briskly, 'I just wanted to let you know. I'd better go in case the doctor's looking for me.'

'Oh, Mum — '

'I know,' Colleen whispered. 'Don't worry, love. I'm fine. Really. I'll let you know when there's any news.'

Sarah sat by the phone, trying to take in Colleen's news, for almost half an hour.

'Anybody home?' her dad's voice called out.

She jumped off the chair, ran into the hall and threw her arms round him.

'Hey — what's all this? Sarah? What's happened?'

'Mum just rang. Tony's had a heart attack.'

'No.' Ralph held his daughter tight for a few moments. 'How's Colleen?'

'That's the funny thing, she seemed quite calm.' They walked into the kitchen. 'It

208

sounds serious, though. When I asked if he was going to be all right, she said the doctors had told her it was too soon to tell.'

'Tony's a blasted fool!' Ralph burst out. 'Even when he's supposed to be enjoying himself, he has to make a mountain out of everything. And this — this obsession with his confounded business — '

'I like him,' Sarah said quietly.

'So do I, but — ' The words seemed to lack sincerity and the sentence was never completed. 'Is Colleen going to call again?'

'As soon as there's any news.' Sarah nodded.

'Then we'll just have to wait, and hope for the best.' He checked his watch. 'I have to go out in an hour, and I'm on call this week. If she rings when I'm not here — Will you be in tonight?'

'Yes. Don't worry, I'll get you on your mobile as soon as there's any news.'

Ralph nodded.

'I hope Mum's all right,' she said softly.

They didn't feel like eating. Sarah made them coffee, but they didn't drink it.

'I can't wait!' Sarah announced suddenly. 'I need to be with her.' She saw her dad's raised eyebrows. 'I don't have anything planned that can't wait a week or so, and I can't bear to think of her going through this alone. I know she's got lots of friends, and Tony's family will be with her, but it's not the same, is it?'

'It's not the same at all.' His voice was gruff as he hugged her.

'Ring the airport, Dad. I'll go and pack a few things . . . '

9

It was snowing — the last snow of this year, the first of next. The night was frosty and clear, and in under two hours, they would be singing 'Auld Lang Syne' and making resolutions. They would make plans for the year. What a waste of time that was when none of them knew what lay ahead.

Most of them had stood here twelve months ago, little knowing that Daisy would be celebrating six months of marriage. And even in her wildest dreams, Megan hadn't imagined *she* would be married . . .

After spending Christmas in Germany with Hans' family, this gathering was a combined Christmas and New Year family celebration.

Snow might be falling, but her parents were discussing summer holiday plans with Hans. Daisy, Andy, Flora and Joy were watching a comedy on television. Hans was busy filling glasses . . .

Daisy and Andy kept exchanging smiles and holding hands. Joy was happy — this time next year, she would have finished with school for ever.

Megan wasn't sure what to make of Flora.

She kept smiling and making jokes, telling them of her life in London, and the new flat she and her friend had moved into, but something didn't ring true. Megan suspected something important was weighing on her daughter's mind.

She followed Hans into the kitchen.

'You make a good waiter.' She helped herself to a handful of peanuts. 'But it might be time to start watering down the sherry. Mum's starting to giggle.'

'I'd noticed.' Laughing, he slipped his arms around her waist. 'And what would my lovely wife like to drink?'

'The truth?' She leaned back against him and he laughed.

'Your wish is my command.' He switched on the kettle and reached for the tea.

She looked through to the sitting-room, where her family were laughing at something on the television.

'Do you think Flora's OK?' she asked Hans.

'In what way?'

'She seems — I don't know, as if there's something on her mind.'

'Ah!' Hans poured the tea and handed her a cup.

'You're very well trained,' she said, kissing him.

'That's me. New Man, or Modern Man — or whatever it is they call us these days.'

'A miracle — that's what I call you. And what did that 'Ah' mean?' she asked with a frown. 'It sounded a very knowing 'Ah'.'

'You said you thought there was something on Flora's mind. I think there's some*one*.'

'Like who?' she asked in astonishment.

'Her boss.'

'Doug? No — she hardly mentions him these days.'

'Exactly. He doesn't mention her, either. Not to me, at any rate.'

'So what makes you think . . . '

'They're seeing quite a bit of each other,' Hans said.

'But that's more professional than personal, surely?'

'Perhaps.'

'Flora and Doug?' Megan frowned. 'No. He's too old for her, for one thing. And for another — oh no, I'm sure you're wrong.'

'Then you'll have to ask Flora,' Hans said.

'I have. She told me I was imagining things.'

'Perhaps you are.' He kissed her, slowly and tenderly. 'Now — much as I'd like to keep you all to myself, I think we ought to go and supervise your mother's sherry intake . . . '

At a few minutes to midnight, Flora turned up the volume on the television and Hans filled everyone's glasses.

The chimes of Big Ben boomed out and cries of 'Happy New Year' echoed through the house. Everyone hugged and kissed, and vowed to stick to their resolutions — then chaos reigned.

Flora broke all records dashing to answer the phone. Megan's friends and neighbours, Jackie and Tom arrived. Daisy and Andy said their goodbyes and set off to join the celebrations at his dad's house. And Rebel barked happily at the pandemonium . . .

'Who was on the phone?' Megan asked Flora.

'Doug — he wished you all a happy new year.'

His phone call had certainly put a smile on Flora's face, and Megan exchanged a thoughtful glance with Hans . . .

★ ★ ★

Sarah jumped to her feet and ran to open the door when she heard Andy's car pull into the drive.

214

'Happy New Year!' She hugged her sister-in-law, waited until Andy had locked the car, then hugged him. 'It's a madhouse here. Mark managed to demolish the Christmas tree, so he and Ben are putting that straight. Jack's got dozens of friends here. Guitars, too, I'm afraid. You should have heard their version of Auld Lang Syne.' She rolled her eyes. 'It would have brought tears to Burns' eyes.'

'Dad not here?' Andy asked.

'He was called out . . .'

Minutes later, Sarah was laughing to herself. Daisy and Andy's arrival had merely added to the chaos.

'I was adjusting the star on the top,' Mark said, telling them how he came to wreck the tree. 'Sarah hadn't got it on straight — it's been bugging me for days — anyway, I sort of overbalanced and fell on top of the tree.'

'And you're planning to be a surgeon?' Andy pulled a face at Daisy. 'Don't ever let him loose on me.'

Mark laughed, and Sarah was relieved. Her brother hadn't been at his most cheerful during the holiday. He and Carol were seeing each other now and again but, reading between the lines, Sarah gathered that Carol was also seeing a lot of Brad.

215

The phone rang and Sarah went to the kitchen, the only place she was likely to hear their caller.

'Happy New Year, darling!'

'Mum!' A huge lump came to her throat.

Colleen rang every year, at more or less the same time, but this year things were so different.

Six months ago, following her mum's phone call, Sarah had dashed off to California thinking she would keep Colleen company until Tony was well again.

She could still see her mum's face — Tony had died a couple of hours before.

Even now, Sarah found it hard to believe he was gone. He'd been so energetic, so lively, and so young . . .

'How are you?' she asked.

'Me? Fine. What are you all doing?'

She wasn't 'fine'. How could she be?

Sarah had spent three weeks in California and Colleen had hit rock bottom. They'd grown very close, but since Sarah's return to England, the phone calls were always the same. Colleen insisted she was fine . . .

'Dad was called out,' she said. 'I'll get him to call you when he comes in.'

'No need, love. Just wish him a happy new year from me.'

'What are *you* doing?' Sarah asked quietly.

'A couple of friends are coming round later,' Colleen said lightly, but Sarah suspected she was lying.

'Have a word with everyone — I'll talk to you again when they've finished, so don't ring off . . .'

Sarah waited patiently while Colleen spoke to her sons and daughter-in-law.

'I'm glad you're having a good time,' she said when Sarah finally got on the line again.

'It would be better if you were here, Mum. I wish you'd come home.'

'I am home, love. But I'll come for a holiday, just as soon as the lawyers have sorted things out.'

'When will that be?' Sarah wanted to pin her to a date.

'Isn't that the sixty-four dollar question!' Colleen sighed. 'I don't know. These things don't move quickly, I know that. At times, they don't seem to move at all.' There was a pause. 'Anyway, I'd better go. Don't forget to wish your dad a happy new year from me.'

'I won't. And you promise you'll come for a holiday?'

'Of course — just as soon as the lawyers have finished.'

'But you don't need to be there, do you? Surely they can sort things out?'

'It's complicated,' Colleen told her. 'But I'll be in touch, Sarah. I love you.'

Sarah returned to the celebrations, but it was hard to be cheerful when her mother was alone.

When Jack's friends finally left, everything slowed down. Ben left and, soon afterwards, one by one, everyone else gave up and went to bed.

Sarah was tired, but she wasn't sleepy. She sat in the sitting-room with just the glow of the tree lights for company.

Ralph's car pulled into the driveway and Sarah went to open the door for him. It was still snowing lightly, but it wasn't making much impression on the roads.

'You still partying?' he asked with a smile.

'No. Everyone else has gone to bed.' She shut the door behind them. 'Happy New Year, Dad.'

'Happy New Year, love.' He kissed her and shrugged off his coat. 'You OK?' he asked with a curious frown.

'Yes, but Mum rang.'

'How did she sound?'

'How can you tell on the phone? She said she had friends visiting later, but I didn't believe her.' There was no point telling him that she thought her mum had hung up in tears. She probably hadn't. It was probably

218

her imagination. 'Do you want a real drink, or a coffee?'

'I'd better have a coffee in case I'm called out again.'

Ralph walked into the sitting-room and dropped into a chair. It had been a long, busy night and he was exhausted. He ought to be getting some sleep instead of scowling at the Christmas tree.

Every year was the same: he dreaded the sight of the decorations. Thankfully, the tree lights he and Colleen had bought for their first Christmas had been thrown out years ago, but he still spent the entire time looking forward to twelfth night, when the decorations returned to the loft for another year. The festivities always came with a reminder that something was missing from their lives. And this year had been worse than most. Normally, he'd had the consolation that his ex-wife had made her choice and was happy. This year, he hadn't even had that . . .

'Mum said to wish you a happy new year.' Sarah came into the room and put the tray on the table. 'I said I'd get you to give her a ring, but she said there was no need. You will ring her, though, won't you?'

'Yes.' He glanced at his watch. 'It's not a new year over there yet. I'll ring later.'

He gave his daughter the best smile he could manage. 'You can't expect her to sound happy, Sarah. Christmas and New Year is a bad time for anyone who's lost someone close. Seeing everyone else enjoying themselves just makes things worse.'

'I know.' She poured their coffee and helped herself to a biscuit. 'I tried to persuade her to come home — she said she *was* home.'

'She is, love. She's lived most of her adult life over there.'

'But it's not the same, is it?'

'She has her life over there. Friends. Family.'

'*Tony's* family,' Sarah said. 'She said he was jealous of you,' she added quietly. 'It was the day after he died, and she wasn't making much sense, but she said he resented the way she turned to you with her problems. Apparently, they'd argued about it not long before he died. When they were in England, I suppose.' She took another biscuit from the plate. 'But what does it matter now? She shouldn't be over there on her own, Dad. Can't you talk to her?'

'And say what?' Ralph picked up his coffee. 'If there was anything I could say, I'd say it. But there isn't. She's a grown woman, Sarah. She has to make her own choices.'

'You could persuade her to visit.'

'I could try,' he corrected her. 'And I will. But don't expect much. Colleen will do what she wants to do, what she feels is right.'

'I suppose so.'

They drank their coffee in a thoughtful silence.

'Aren't we cheerful on this bright new year,' Ralph said with a wry smile.

'Things can only get better.' Chuckling, Sarah rose to her feet. 'I'm off to bed. I'll see you in the morning.'

'I'll ring your mum and then I'll head for bed. Hopefully, I won't be called out again . . .'

Ralph was too distracted to reach for the phone. Had Tony been jealous of him? Strange to think of two men, both jealous of the other. Perhaps Colleen had brought her problems to him more than she should. Perhaps he'd encouraged her to . . .

He switched off the tree lights and pulled back the curtain. It had stopped snowing, leaving just a thin covering on the ground.

As he stood there, staring out at the silent world, he tried to think of some way he could persuade Colleen to come home. Despite everything he'd said to Sarah, a faint hope flickered. He might succeed.

He returned to his chair, held the phone

on his lap and punched out her number.

It rang for a long time, and he was about to replace the receiver when she finally answered.

All she said was 'Hello?', but it was a very empty sound.

'It's only me,' he said lightly. 'I'm sorry I missed your call.'

'What time is it over there? Are you still celebrating?'

'No, the party was over when I got in. Sarah was still up and we sat talking for a while.' He paused. 'She's worried about you, Colleen.'

'There's no need,' she said with a heavy sigh.

'There's every need,' he argued gently. 'If you'd just come over for a visit — '

'You know I can't, Ralph.'

'Colleen, you can't keep using the lawyers as an excuse.' He took a deep breath and spoke more calmly. 'You've been through a lot. Why suffer alone when you could be with your family? That's what families are for.'

'And make you suffer, too?' she asked softly. 'No, Ralph. Tony always said I ran straight to you if I had a problem. He was right. It's high time I learned to stand on my own two feet.'

'Rubbish!' Ralph scoffed. 'The only

problems have been connected to the children, either directly or indirectly. You're the mother of my children, Colleen. Why the devil shouldn't you turn to me?'

'Ralph — tell Sarah I'm fine.'

'She's not a kid any more,' he reminded her. 'And it's not just Sarah. We're all worried about you. We all want you here.'

'I'll come for a couple of weeks in the summer,' she said briskly. 'Now, forget about me. Tell me about Christmas.'

'If you'd been here — '

'Ralph!' But there was a hint of amusement in her voice, so he told her every detail of their Christmas, as he'd done so many times before . . .

When the call ended, he drew back the curtains and stood looking out until a small patch of light appeared in the sky.

The world slowly came to life. Cars drove past, covered in a sprinkling of white. Their neighbour, wrapped up to ward off the cold, walked his dog towards the park.

'Dad?'

Ralph spun round at the sound of Sarah's voice.

'You're up early.'

'And you're up late.' She frowned at him. 'You look dreadful — you've been here all night!'

223

'There didn't seem much point going to bed,' he answered lamely.

'You rang Mum?' she asked, and he nodded.

'She seemed — OK.'

'OK enough to have you fretting about her all night?' she asked dryly. She came into the room and switched on the tree lights. 'That's better. Let's have some breakfast.'

Ralph followed her into the kitchen, but she seemed to have forgotten breakfast. She was looking at him with a very thoughtful expression on her face.

'Something wrong?' he asked curiously.

'You and Mum,' she began slowly. 'You've always told us that you both agreed on everything — like us staying here with you, when we visited Mum and that sort of thing — and I know it was all very amicable. But — well, what about the divorce?'

'What about it?' Ralph frowned, not understanding. 'It was all very — amicable.'

'Yes, but Mum wanted it, didn't she? You loved her when you married her. Presumably, you still loved her when you got divorced?'

'Yes,' he answered slowly. 'I still loved her.'

'That must have been awful, Dad.'

'No.' The lie came easily. 'At least I had you children, and so long as I had you, I had a link to your mother.' He filled the kettle. 'I don't know about you, but I'm ready for my first breakfast of the year.'

Sarah might not have heard him.

'When did you stop loving her, Dad?'

The question caught him off guard, and his expression must have answered for him.

'You never did, did you?' she asked softly.

Ralph didn't answer directly.

'I was thinking,' he said instead, 'that I might go over and see her — you know, face to face. I've got a lot of leave owing. I'll see if she's coping as well as she says she is.

'I won't let her know, I'll just arrive.' He gave her a wry smile. 'She always claims she likes surprises . . .'

★ ★ ★

Flora had been back at work for three days when she reached the depressing conclusion that Doug was avoiding her.

She stayed behind long after everyone had gone home. Everyone except Doug, that is. He was always first to arrive and last to leave.

She sat outside his office, and listened to the muffled sound of his voice as he made several phone calls.

Her patience was rewarded just before

seven-thirty. He was putting on his jacket as he emerged from his office, but he stopped when he saw her.

'You waiting for me?'

'Yes.' She gathered up the papers she'd been reading. 'I stayed later than I planned. I wondered if I could cadge a lift home.'

'Of course.' He began striding along the corridor and Flora had to break into a trot to catch him up.

He gave the lift a cursory glance and headed for the stairs. Flora remembered her mum's engagement party, all those months ago, when Doug had kissed her in the hotel's lift. She wondered if he was remembering, too. If he was, he wasn't finding it a particularly pleasant memory . . .

'You're not going down with this flu bug, I hope,' he said. 'You look a bit pale.'

'I feel fine.' She'd been feeling fuzzy-headed all day, but she didn't think she was getting flu. By all accounts, the bug that was currently knocking down the staff like flies started with a raging headache and a bad cold.

'Would you like to get something to eat?' she asked when she was sitting beside him in his car.

'No, thanks. I really can't spare the time.'

'Tomorrow?'

'No, Flora.'

For once, there was little traffic on the roads to hold them up.

'So you're planning to keep on ignoring me?' she asked.

'That's ridiculous.' He sighed loudly. 'How could I do that when we work in the same building?'

'You'd think it would be tricky,' she answered airily, 'but you seem to be succeeding.'

'I've been busy, you've been busy. We've had nothing to discuss.' He shrugged.

'I take it this is a new year resolution — no more mixing business with pleasure?'

'I told you, Flora, it never works.' He drove away from a crossing. 'I could give you a dozen examples. It just causes — problems.'

'We seemed to be managing OK,' she said. 'We saw each other several times before Christmas. It had nothing to do with business, and it didn't cause problems. You rang me at New Year. That wasn't business. That didn't cause problems.'

'It would, given time.' He turned the car into her road with obvious relief.

'I suppose there's no point asking you in,' Flora said quietly.

'No — thanks. I'll see you tomorrow.'

'I doubt it,' she answered with a sigh . . .

The following morning, Flora woke with a headache that refused to budge and by the end of the day — a day Doug had spent out of the office — her eyes were streaming. The flu had claimed yet another victim.

Flora did nothing but lie in bed with her aches and pains. Her head ached, her limbs ached, even her teeth ached. One minute she felt she was being roasted alive, the next she was huddled above the radiator, with her duvet wrapped round her, shivering until her teeth chattered.

But by far the worst symptom was the melancholy that settled around her. She missed her work, she missed Doug, and twice she burst into tears for no good reason.

She thought Doug might have called to see how she was, but she should have known better. There was no sign of him.

Any hope that he might also have been struck down with the flu and had been too ill to call was dashed when, having suffered for seven days, she returned to work. She met him in the corridor, looking his usual healthy self.

'Are you feeling — ' He scowled at her pale face, and the dark smudges circling her eyes. 'You don't look better. What's the point of coming back before you're fully recovered? All you'll do is give it to the rest of us!'

She'd thought she was better, but as soon as she felt the familiar sting of tears in her eyes, she began to wonder.

'Hey, Flora, I didn't mean — ' He lifted her chin and frowned at the shimmer of tears in her eyes. 'I just meant you shouldn't have come back until you're feeling back to normal. As for giving it to everyone else, I think I'm the only person who's escaped it.' He smiled, but there was no answering smile from Flora. 'Would you like me to take you home?' he asked.

She shook her head; she couldn't answer for the huge lump in her throat.

The morning was spent at her desk. She didn't see Doug which, judging from rumours flying around about the mood he was in, was just as well. Then, when she did seek him out, she was told he'd gone to lunch.

She spent her own lunchbreak composing a letter. When she was satisfied, she printed it, and left it on his desk.

Her phone rang just after two-thirty.

'I want you in my office now!' he bellowed down the line at her, and she winced at the crash of his receiver being banged down.

She set off for his office, and was surprised

to meet him striding furiously along the corridor towards her.

'I thought you wanted — '

'Get your coat,' he snapped. 'I'm taking you home.'

'I'm perfectly — '

'You're not perfectly anything!' He grabbed her arm and led her to her coat. He even helped her put it on. 'As soon as I saw you this morning, I knew you shouldn't have been here.'

They were in the corridor, and he gave her a push in the direction of the lift.

'And no, I won't accept your resignation,' he told her, as he hit the button to close the doors. 'I have never heard anything so ridiculous, not to mention downright childish, in my life.'

The lift took them to the ground floor and Flora thought that perhaps he was right. Perhaps she had come back too soon. She was feeling decidedly weepy again.

'And don't even think about coming back till next week,' he warned her as they headed for his car. 'You won't be allowed on the premises.'

As he drove her home, she wondered what had prompted her to tender her resignation from a job she loved, when all she wanted to do was burst into tears and sleep for a fortnight. Hardly the actions of someone at their best.

Doug stopped the car outside her building, switched off the engine and unfastened his seatbelt.

'I'm inviting myself in for a coffee,' he explained, seeing her surprised expression.

Flora let them into her flat and switched on the heaters. She was heading for the kitchen to make coffee when he stopped her.

'You don't look as if you've got enough strength to hold a spoon.' He nodded towards the sitting-room. 'Go and sit down.'

As he clattered around in the kitchen, Flora pulled up a chair by the heater and curled up in it. She felt a little foolish, as well as embarrassed by her rash behaviour.

'Where are the — It's OK, I've found them.' After more clattering, he called out, 'I assume you do have — Got it!'

Minutes later, he brought coffee into the room. It looked a lot stronger than Flora felt.

'Your letter of resignation,' Doug said, sitting opposite her. 'What was that in aid of?'

'I thought if we no longer worked together — '

'It would change nothing, Flora.'

'So this nonsense about not mixing business with pleasure is just an excuse?'

231

she demanded, hurt.

'No. I don't think it's a good idea.' He gazed into her angry face. 'But regardless of whether we work together — just look at us, Flora. I'm sixteen years older than you.'

'So?'

'So I was sixteen when you were born. I was twenty-one when you went off to school for the first time.'

'So what?'

'When you're thirty, I shall be forty-six.' He looked at her, saw she was unconvinced, and sighed. 'Perhaps that doesn't sound too bad, but when you're forty, I shall be fifty-six. When you're — '

'Maths might not be my forte, Doug, but I did grasp the basics!' She rose from her chair and walked to the window. 'First, you don't want to mix business and pleasure. Now, you think I'm too young for you. What will it be next?' She turned to face him. 'If we didn't work in the same building, and if I was a decade or so older, would you be interested or would you come up with some other flimsy excuse?'

'If you were thinking rationally, you'd know — '

'Why don't you just tell me the truth? Why not just tell me you're not interested?'

'Because it wouldn't be true. You know

232

it wouldn't.' He stood in front of her and clasped her hands in his. 'Perhaps working together wouldn't cause too many problems, or none we couldn't handle, but we can't escape the fact that I'm sixteen years older than you.'

'That's not important,' she said urgently.

'It is, Flora!' He released her hands. 'Drink your coffee. There's no point discussing it at the moment — you're not yourself . . .'

He left soon afterwards and Flora crawled into bed.

The following Monday, Flora was on her way back to work, fully recovered.

As she drove past the newsagent's she saw a window full of balloons.

With a sudden laugh, she drove round the corner, parked her car and ran back for a closer look.

'Can you deliver?' she asked the man behind the counter, and he raised his eyebrows.

'Well, I suppose . . .'

Flora quickly wrote down the address before he changed his mind . . .

* * *

Hans was studying the restaurant's menu when Doug arrived. He thought his friend looked more harassed than usual, but he knew that with a magazine like *En Passant* to run, it was difficult not to.

'Have you ordered?' Doug sat opposite him.

'No, I've only been here a couple of minutes.'

'I'm not complaining — it's high time you bought me lunch — but is there a reason for this?'

'No reason,' Hans lied. 'I had time to kill before a late afternoon appointment.' He could hardly say that Megan had asked him to quiz Doug about Flora. 'And I must owe you a lunch.'

'Oh, at least one,' Doug agreed, smiling.

Their food was being put in front of them when Doug asked after Megan. Hans grabbed the opportunity.

'She's great. Well — she's a bit worried about Flora, actually.'

'I don't think anyone needs to worry about Flora,' Doug retorted. 'She's tougher than the rest of us put together.'

'I know.' Hans had to smile, but he wasn't sure what to make of Doug's expression. 'You know what mothers are like, though. And Flora has seemed very low. It's unlike her.'

'The flu bug's knocked everyone down,

and it seemed to affect Flora more than most. But she's back at her desk — fully recovered.'

Which told Hans nothing.

'Getting on all right, are you?' he asked.

'Professionally, you mean? Yes, fine.'

'And on a personal level?'

Doug looked at him for long moments.

'On a personal level, she's driving me mad.' He put down his knife and fork. 'We started seeing quite a lot of each other, as you know. That was my fault, I suppose. It's always a mistake when two people who work together start getting too involved. But when I tried to tell Flora that, she handed in her notice.'

'She did what?' Hans said in amazement.

'She had flu. She wasn't thinking straight,' Doug dismissed this. 'But I've tried to make her see sense, Hans. Apart from everything else, I'm sixteen years her senior — practically old enough to be her father.' He picked up his knife and fork again. 'At the moment, I don't know whether I'm coming or going.'

'I see.'

'You don't,' Doug assured him with a sigh. 'She refuses to listen. I only saw her briefly this morning — she asked if I needed help crossing the road, then dropped a fifty pence piece into my hand, saying it was her contribution to Help the Aged.'

Hans gave a deep rumble of laughter.

'That's just the way she is, Doug. And she clearly doesn't see an age gap as a problem. She's very sensible, mature, young — '

'Mature?' Doug grimaced. 'Mid-way through the morning, I had a delivery of balloons.'

'Balloons?'

'Two dozen of the things. Enormous, heart-shaped balloons. All identical. One side says 'I love you' and the other — ' He scowled at Hans. 'Oh, yes, very funny.'

'Sorry.'

'At least you can put Megan's mind at rest, I suppose. Her daughter is well and truly back on form. In danger of being sent on an assignment to darkest Peru,' he muttered darkly, 'but back to her old self.'

'I'm glad.' Hans couldn't help his laughter.

'Whatever will she dream up next?' Doug gave a reluctant smile. 'What am I going to do with her, Hans?'

'I don't know. But it seems to me that your life would be very dull without her.'

'I liked it when life was dull!'

'Did you?'

Doug shrugged, but he didn't answer.

'I used to think you were the most determined, stubborn person I knew.' Hans laughed softly. 'Then I met Flora . . . '

236

10

Ralph sat back as the taxi sped towards Colleen's address. On his few previous visits to America, talkative drivers had simply been another aspect of the country he'd taken for granted. Now, just when he would have welcomed questions about life in little old England, he had the misfortune to hire the quietest driver in America.

He tried to take in the amazing sights of San Francisco, but none of it meant anything.

Leicestershire had been nestling prettily in a white coating of frost when he left. Sunshine had sparkled on every frozen blade of grass. It had been one of those perfect days — blue sky and bright sunshine. California might have been a distant planet.

It had taken him weeks to plan this visit, to make sure there was someone to cover for him at the surgery, but now he was here, he had no idea what he was going to say to Colleen. At home, surrounded by familiarity, it had made perfect sense. Now, any words that sprang to mind sounded arrogant and presumptuous.

He wished the children were with him. It was the first time he'd made this journey without one or more of them with him . . .

The taxi came to a stop outside a house Ralph didn't recognise. Colleen and Tony had bought it four years ago, and he'd never seen it. A large front lawn, the same as those belonging to surrounding properties, ran down to the road.

'Enjoy your stay,' the driver said, putting Ralph's suitcase on the pavement.

'Thanks.' He'd thought of asking the driver to wait, in case Colleen wasn't home, but he could easily get another to take him to the nearest hotel.

He picked up his case and began walking up the sweeping driveway to the imposing front door.

'Ralph!'

Colleen's anguished cry stopped him in his tracks. She stood at the open door, her hand against her heart.

'Everything's fine,' he said hastily. 'The children are fine. I just wanted to — surprise you.'

'Surprise me?' she cried. 'Ralph, how could you? You frightened me to death!'

'Sorry.' This wasn't what he'd planned. 'You always turn up out of the blue,' he reminded her lamely. 'You say you like surprises.'

'But I don't have the children, do I?' she snapped.

'Sorry,' Ralph said again, but she was striding inside, leaving him to follow.

He left his suitcase in the hall and followed her into a large sitting-room that was dotted with white chairs and rugs. The room was so impersonal it reminded him of his surgery.

'What are you doing here, Ralph?' She stood in the centre of the room, tapping her foot on the polished wood floor. Her hands were trembling, he noticed.

The dress she was wearing, in warm shades of gold, seemed to draw attention to her pale face. She'd always been slim, but the weight she'd lost since Ralph had last seen her made her look unwell.

'You can't stay here,' she added, her voice rising.

'Why not?' His heart ached to see her in this cold, heartless room. She looked totally lost and out of her depth. 'Are you worried what the neighbours might think?' he asked with a smile. 'We have four children, Colleen.'

'What are you doing here?' She didn't smile. 'I suppose Sarah's behind this? Every time I speak to her, she nags me to pack up and go home.' She threw out her arms. 'This is my home. It has been for years.'

'She's worried about you and she wants you — home. Is that so terrible?' He took a step towards her, but she took a step back. He decided to try a different approach.

'Back home,' he said teasingly, 'we have this custom. We offer visitors coffee. I suppose over here it's iced tea or some such thing.'

'Would you like some iced tea?' A reluctant smile tugged at her lips.

'Not on your life.' Ralph pulled a face. 'I'll have a coffee, though, if there's any going.'

She nodded and walked past him. They went through the hall, where she looked at his suitcase.

'You can't stay here.'

'That's OK. I'll check into a hotel. Can you recommend one where the staff don't say 'Have a nice day' every five minutes?'

'There are plenty.' She almost managed another smile, but not quite.

While she made coffee, Ralph looked around him. The kitchen was fitted out with every labour-saving device imaginable. A photographer could have captured it, just as it was, for a glossy interior design magazine.

He could picture his own kitchen. The table would be piled high with Sarah's fabrics — despite having a room of her own, she did most of her work in the kitchen.

Tea and coffee cups would be scattered on every surface. Jack's school books would be balanced on the window ledges or on top of the washing machine.

Long-out-of-date notes would be stuck on the fridge door. Postcards would be pinned on the cork board for all to see . . .

Ralph's house might not win any awards, but it was a home. Here, nothing was out of place. It looked as if the residents had moved out.

Colleen's hands were shaking so violently that the cups clattered alarmingly against the saucers.

'How are the lawyers getting on?' he asked. 'You're OK, aren't you? I mean financially?' He could see she wasn't OK in any other way.

'Yes. I told you — Tony was always careful about that sort of thing. He often joked that he was worth more dead than alive.' She gave a deep shuddering sigh at the memory. 'I can live here in splendour for as long as I like.'

'Splendour?'

'Don't you like it?' She handed him a cup of coffee.

'Not really,' he replied. 'It's too — hygienic, pristine, tidy.'

'It doesn't have four children messing it up,' she said with a fond smile. 'The first time the children visited us, Jack would have been — what? Four?'

'Five.' Ralph sat at the gleaming white table.

'He'd just started school,' Colleen remembered. 'That house was much smaller than this, but we'd spent a fortune having it decorating. Then Jack wrote his name on every wall with non-washable crayons.' She sat down at the table, a wistful smile on her face. 'It was ages before I could bring myself to cover up his efforts.'

Ralph watched as the memories flitted across her face. She'd missed so much of her children's lives. He only hoped the sacrifice had been worth it.

He was lucky. Sarah and Jack were still at home. Mark might live in London, but he still called their house 'home', and Andy and Daisy were regular visitors.

Colleen, on the other hand, had nothing but this empty house. The thought was more than Ralph could bear.

'I'm taking you home, Colleen.'

Her head snapped up.

'I am home, Ralph! I keep telling — '

'This isn't home,' he scoffed. 'This is — '

'No.' She was on her feet, pacing the room. 'I intend to stand on my own two feet, just for once,' she said. 'I can't keep turning to you, Ralph. Tony always said — ' But she didn't finish the sentence. 'My friends are here. My life is here. I need to do this on my own. I need to sort things out with the lawyers. Then I thought I'd sell this house.

'I shall probably get a job, too, and make a new life for myself. It won't be easy — first I had you to lean on, then Tony . . . and he said I still leaned on you . . . I might be struggling at the moment, but I'll get there in the end . . .'

Her hands covered her face, and huge sobs shook her body.

Ralph was beside her in an instant, holding her close. Slowly, very slowly, she took her hands from her face and linked them around his neck. She cried and cried, clinging to him as if she would never let him go.

Ralph said nothing. He stroked her hair, and made the occasional soothing noise, but he said nothing. There would be time enough to talk later.

Ralph suspected she hadn't cried since Tony died. At the time, she would have put on a brave face for Sarah's sake. She'd always been hard on herself, too, always determined to put on a bright smile . . .

Later, Ralph cooked omelettes and Colleen laughed. Her eyes were still red and swollen from crying, but her laughter was a wonderful sound.

'This reminds me of when we were first married,' she said. 'You could only cook omelettes — remember? And I couldn't even manage that. Remember all those cookery classes I went to . . . ?'

Ralph encouraged her to reminisce and she began to relax.

He rang Sarah and when he'd finished, Colleen was fast asleep in the chair. He hunted upstairs for a blanket, covered her up, and left her there to enjoy her much-needed sleep. Then he went to one of the spare bedrooms, stretched out on the bed, and slept.

The next morning, he was making himself coffee when Colleen joined him. She still looked tired, but at least she was more relaxed.

'How long are you staying?' she asked suddenly. 'Long enough to do some sight-seeing?'

'That depends on you. I'm not leaving without you, Colleen.'

'Ralph — '

'My biggest mistake was letting you go in the first place.' He chose his words with care. 'I thought ours was everything a marriage should be, but it wasn't, was it? Not for

244

you, at any rate. I was too wrapped up in everything else — job, kids — to see what it was doing to you.'

'Please, don't, Ralph. It's ancient history. Nothing we say can change anything now. It's all in the past.'

She was right; the past had gone. But he so wanted a future for them . . .

'You belong in England,' he said carefully. 'You have friends there. Megan's always asking after you and I know you speak on the phone often. And the kids need you, Colleen. They always have.

'Oh, they're getting on with their lives, they're independent, but they still need you. Mark will soon qualify as a doctor, Jack will probably end up wearing a dog collar and, in a few years, I expect Andy will be a father. What will any of that be like for them, when their mother's on the other side of the world?'

Colleen didn't answer, she was blinking back tears.

'What about Sarah?' Ralph asked. 'She and Ben are crazy about each other. I wouldn't be surprised if he hadn't asked her to marry him already, but when she says yes, Sarah will want it all — career, husband, home, children. And she'll want her mother. She always has.'

Colleen walked to the window, wrapping her arms round herself.

'But this has nothing to do with the children, Colleen. This has to do with us — and I'm not leaving without you.'

She turned to look at him, and he saw a host of questions in her eyes.

'I have never stopped loving you, Colleen . . .'

★ ★ ★

'Mark!' Flora gave an exasperated laugh. 'You're not listening to a word I'm saying.'

'I am!' He dragged his eyes away from a spot just behind Flora's right shoulder.

Flora turned to look. A pretty blonde-headed girl was staring unhappily into a mug of coffee.

'Do you know her?' Flora asked curiously. 'Or are you just indulging in a bit of wishful thinking?'

'I know her — sort of.' Mark nodded. 'Her name's Victoria and she's training to be a doctor. She's a year behind me.'

'She doesn't look too happy with life. Why not ask her to join us?'

'Would you mind?'

'Of course not.' Flora was surprised and amused by his eager expression.

Flora had been given strict instructions

246

from Sarah to use this lunch date as an information-gathering exercise. She was supposed to be finding out all she could about Mark's relationship with Carol. Mark wasn't giving much away, though.

For the next twenty minutes, Flora might not have existed. Mark and Victoria were so busy commiserating with each other on the hardships a career in the medical profession involved that they didn't notice her.

Flora was intrigued. Wait till she told Sarah!

'She seems nice,' Flora remarked when Victoria had left them.

'Yes. I don't really know her that well, but — yes, she seems nice.'

'She seemed keen on you, too.'

'Do you think so?'

'Definitely.' Flora struggled to keep a straight face.

'I might try and track her down later,' Mark said, with a nonchalant shrug. He glanced at his watch. 'We'd better get cracking if you want to be back by two. I'll walk back with you, if you like.'

They left the coffee bar and walked smartly along the streets.

'Have you heard if Daisy and Andy are coming home this weekend?' she asked.

'I've no idea.' He turned to look at her.

'Are you going home?'

'I wasn't, but I will if they're planning a visit. I shall soon forget what my little sister looks like.'

'Let me know if you hear anything. And I'll let you know. We can go in my car, if you like.'

'OK. Thanks, Mark.' They stopped outside her building and she reached up and kissed him. 'Thanks for lunch, too. If I haven't heard from you, I'll give you a ring on Friday afternoon about the weekend.' She began walking away. 'And give my regards to Victoria,' she added with a teasing laugh . . .

Flora was about to push open the double glass doors when she collided with Doug who was coming from the opposite direction.

'Who was that?' he demanded.

'Who was what?'

'The man you were kissing for all the world to see!' He pushed open the door and stood back to let her pass.

'Jealous?' she asked with a sweet smile.

He didn't answer. He didn't need to; she could see that he was.

A knot of despair tightened inside her. Doug's worries about the sixteen year gap in their ages had seemed so unimportant that she'd as good as dismissed them from her mind.

She'd flirted outrageously with him, convinced that, sooner or later, he would see sense and realise they'd been born for each other. But he refused to see it.

'It was Mark,' she explained as they walked towards the stairs. 'Andy's brother.'

'Oh — right! Family!' His smug satisfaction was infuriating.

'His brother's married to my sister, that's all,' she pointed out. 'We both live in London so we get together quite often.'

'I see.' As well as looking smug, he now looked amused.

'Believe me,' she added for good measure, 'with looks like that, no girl is thinking family when she kisses Mark!'

They'd reached the door and she yanked it open. She marched on, head held high, but when they were level with his office, he put his hand on her arm.

'Would you like to go out tonight?'

'Where?' Her heart was leaping wildly, but she knew there was no point raising her hopes.

'I don't know — we could get something to eat, go dancing, see a show — '

She was busy thinking, and he was in a hurry.

'Think about it,' he said. 'Come along to my office when you finish this afternoon.'

Flora went to her desk and tried to work. But her mind kept coming back to Doug's invitation. Perhaps this time . . . No, they would go out, and Doug would tell her again that the difference in their ages prevented anything but a casual friendship. It would merely prolong the agony.

All the same . . .

He *had* been jealous when he'd seen her with Mark. And he *had* asked her out. It would be the first time in ages they'd spent time together without business getting in the way.

Her computer bleeped again and she tried to turn her mind to the piece she was writing . . .

She vowed to behave like a sensible, mature, serious adult, thus making Doug forget the sixteen years between them. The trouble was, around Doug she didn't feel in the least sensible or mature. Throughout her life she'd been told she was too serious and ambitious but, with Doug, she felt light-hearted and childish, as if the world had been created for their own personal entertainment.

However, when she switched off her computer for the day, and headed for Doug's office, she tried to look mature and sensible.

His door was open. He was talking on the phone and he waved at her to come in.

She stood by the window, looking down at the well-lit street below, as she waited for him to finish his call. A stranger lifted his face, saw her standing at the window and blew her a kiss.

Flora spluttered with laughter and was returning the kiss when she saw Doug's exasperated gaze resting on her.

Smiling, she wriggled around the phone cable and sat on his knee. At which point, he gave up, promising to speak to his caller the following morning.

'Anyone I might know?' he asked, nodding towards the window.

'It was nobody I know.' She linked her arms round his neck. 'And no, I don't normally blow kisses to perfect strangers. Only when they do it first.'

'I see.' He was smiling. 'Do I take it we have a date tonight then?'

'On one condition.'

'What's that?' he asked warily.

'You don't subject me to any of that 'I'm too old for you' nonsense.'

'Deal.' He nodded.

'Really? Good. In that case, perhaps I'll try and convince you that age is just a number. Perhaps I'll convince you that you're wasting time — wasting our futures.'

'Perhaps I'm convinced,' he said quietly.

'Are you?' Her heart raced.

He didn't answer immediately.

'Not entirely,' he said, dashing her hopes. 'I still think sixteen years — '

'It's nothing.' She stood up, putting distance between them. They'd had this argument too many times before. 'People are only as old as they feel. How old do you feel?'

'When I'm around you?' he asked with a wry smile. 'Oh — about twenty.'

'As old as that?' She gave a burst of laughter. 'You make me feel about fourteen.'

'I suppose that only puts six years between us.' He stood up and pulled her close. 'Sixteen years is a lot, Flora. In the future, you might feel — '

'I'll feel exactly the same!'

'I hope so.' He brushed her hair from her face. 'Because I know I shall.'

'You mean — '

'I mean,' he said, smiling at her, 'that I don't approve, and I'm sure your mother won't approve, but — ' He paused to kiss her, then gazed at her with a slight frown on his face. 'I hate the thought of you not being in my life. I hate the thought of you being in someone else's life. And I hate the thought of spending the rest of my life wondering what might have been.'

'I love you so much,' Flora said urgently.

'I love you, too.'

As they kissed, all Flora could think was that he loved her. Nothing else mattered. She had known, deep down, but she had thought she might never hear him say it . . .

He loved her. Those three words would carry her through anything that life might put her way.

'You are so stubborn,' she murmured.

'I'm sorry, but — '

'Don't. We'll never mention our ages again,' she said firmly. 'We're young and in love, that's all that matters.'

'Shall we spend the weekend in Paris?' he asked.

'Oh, let's!' She gave a delighted laugh. 'That is so romantic!'

Laughing, Doug reached for her hand and began walking to the door.

'I'll be far more romantic when I've eaten,' he told her. 'Come on.'

'And afterwards, we'll dance until dawn,' she said dreamily.

'You speak for yourself,' he retorted with a grin. 'I'm far too old for that sort of thing . . .'

★ ★ ★

Megan hurried downstairs and was about to start preparing breakfast when she decided to call Sarah first.

Ever since Joy had persuaded Sarah to take care of Rebel for the week, Megan had been feeling guilty. She and Hans were spending a week in Germany, Joy was on a school trip to France, and poor Sarah had knocked on their door just as they'd been deciding Rebel's accommodation.

She punched out Sarah's number.

'Sarah — it's Megan. Just thought I'd see if you were coping.'

'Yes, of course I am. Rebel's fine. He's wolfed down his breakfast and been for a walk. Stop worrying, Megan. What time's your plane?'

'Not for hours yet. And you're sure he's no trouble?'

'None at all,' Sarah said. 'To be honest, I'm glad of the company. Jack comes and goes, but that's it at the moment.'

Megan knew how that felt. Whenever Hans was away, she found the house terribly quiet. She still wasn't used to Daisy being in Manchester, or Flora in London.

'You haven't heard when your dad's coming back?'

'No. I tried ringing last night, but they must have been out.'

'I spoke to your mum on Friday,' Megan told her, 'and she said they'd been sight-seeing. She's really enjoying Ralph's visit. It's doing her good.'

'I hope so,' Sarah murmured.

So did Megan.

'You're sure you're all right?' she said again, and Sarah laughed.

'Yes — stop worrying. If Joy hadn't bullied me into having him, I would have volunteered. Now, go and catch that plane. And have a lovely time . . .'

Hans came into the kitchen just as Megan was replacing the receiver.

'Sarah,' she told him, lifting her face for his kiss.

'Problems?'

'No, I just thought I'd check. She's fine, Rebel's fine.' She smiled up at him.

'Good.' He laughed softly. 'Although, I bet Joy's already wondering how best to convince Sarah that she'd love to adopt one of the strays from the kennels.'

'Don't.'

Megan groaned with amusement.

They'd eaten breakfast, and were having a quick coffee when the phone rang.

'I thought I might have missed you,' Daisy said.

'Hello, love. Everything all right?'

'Great. I just wanted to wish you a good trip. Andy's just left, but he sends his love . . .'

They chatted for a few minutes, then Megan did the washing-up while Hans put their suitcases in the car.

The phone rang again and Megan reached for it.

'Hi, Mum. Just thought I'd wish you bon voyage,' Flora's cheerful voice greeted her.

'Anyone would think we were emigrating,' Megan said with a chuckle, 'instead of visiting family for a week.' She pulled one of the chairs nearer to the phone and sat down. 'You not at work yet?'

'Yes, we came in early. Doug had people to meet at eight-thirty.'

'And Doug's OK?' Megan asked.

'Yes, he's OK.'

'What does OK mean?' she asked with a worried frown. 'You're still — together, aren't you?'

'Of course,' Flora retorted with an exasperated laugh. 'You asked if he was OK — he is. What else can I say?' Her voice softened as she asked, 'You do like him, don't you, Mum? You said you did — before. And Hans likes him.'

'Of course I like him,' she assured Flora quickly. 'I just thought — well, you never know these days. One minute, couples are madly in love, the next, it's all over.

'I was just being nosy. I like to know what's going on.'

'In that case — ' There was amusement in Flora's voice. 'I'm not supposed to be telling you this, and there's no time to discuss it because you'll miss your plane, but we've decided on June for a wedding.

'It will be a small one,' she added quickly. 'Neither of us wants any fuss or frills so there won't be all the palaver there was with Daisy's . . . '

'Flora! How can you tell me this — now?'

'We'll talk when you get back,' Flora promised, laughing.

'You'll come for the weekend? And bring Doug?'

'That sounds good. I'll tell him. Must dash. Give my love to Hans, and have a good time . . . '

★ ★ ★

'It's time we left, darling.' Hans smiled indulgently at his wife who was still holding the phone. 'There's no time for last minute calls.'

'Flora just rang. You'll never guess . . . '

As he ushered her out to the car, she told

257

him about Flora's phone call.

'I'm not surprised,' he said, backing the car out of the drive.

'I am!' The radio was on and she switched it off. 'Flora's always been a bit — well, sceptical about marriage. It's all right in it's place, and a perfect solution for everyone she knows, but she would never let it interfere with her career.

'And then there's Doug,' she went on. 'He's been a bachelor for so long — you'd think he'd want to give the matter a lot of thought.'

'I'm sure he has.' Hans took his eyes from the road briefly and smiled at her. 'You're pleased, aren't you?'

'Oh, yes. Just surprised. It's all a bit sudden.' She smiled happily. 'I'm more than pleased. I'm delighted. Flora's always tended to take herself too seriously. It's strange — they're both very serious, very ambitious, but put them together and there's not a serious thought between them . . . '

The traffic was heavy on the road to the airport, but Hans was soon turning into the car park.

They were walking towards the terminal building when Megan stopped in her tracks. She stared in amazement at the couple some distance away who were walking in

258

the opposite direction.

'Colleen?' But she was too far away. Megan's heels clattered on the tarmac as she ran. 'Colleen!'

This time, Colleen heard her.

'Megan!' With a laugh, she ran to meet Megan. 'What on earth are you doing here?'

'Me? Hans and I are off to Germany for a week.' She hugged her friend tight. 'But what are *you* doing here?'

'I've come home,' Colleen answered, with a self-conscious smile.

'That's wonderful! And you look wonderful.' Megan laughed. 'I can't get over this. I was only speaking to Sarah this morning. She's going to have the surprise of her life!'

Ralph came over to them and Megan hugged him briefly.

'Welcome back, Ralph. You're looking fit.'

He looked better than she'd ever seen him, and Megan knew it had nothing to do with California, holidays or anything else.

At last, Ralph had the woman he loved by his side . . .

Hans was still carrying their suitcases when he joined them. Everyone was talking at once.

'When do you get back?' Colleen asked.

'Next Tuesday,' Megan said. 'Keep that

day free and we'll get together. I have so much to tell you. I am so glad you're home.'

'Me, too,' Colleen said with feeling.

'Megan — we'll miss our plane.' Hans caught Ralph's eye and grinned. 'There are phones, darling . . . '

'I'm coming.' She hugged Colleen again. 'See you Tuesday . . . '

She and Hans began walking towards the terminal building again.

'What a surprise. I can't get over it.' Pausing to look round, she saw Colleen slip her arm through Ralph's. Then Ralph bent his head to catch what she said . . .

'Megan?' Hans' concerned voice broke through and she realised she could see nothing for a blur of tears.

'I'm feeling all emotional,' she admitted with a shaky laugh. 'I am so happy for Colleen. At first, I thought she was just visiting. But when she said she'd come home, she wasn't thinking of England at all.

'I know exactly what she meant — it's how I feel, every time I look at you. As if I've come home.'

'My darling girl.' Hans dropped their suitcases and took her in his arms. 'I feel just the same,' he said gently. 'And it will be how Daisy feels when she's with Andy.

How Flora feels when she's with Doug.'

Smiling, he dropped a gentle kiss on her lips.

'And I expect it will be how Joy will feel when she gets back from France and collects her precious Rebel . . . '

'Rebel!' Megan clapped a hand to her forehead.

'Ah — Ralph and Colleen don't know, do they?' Chuckling, Hans glanced at his watch. 'They soon will — and there's not a thing we can do about it.'

'If Sarah's going to have the surprise of her life,' Megan said with a laugh, 'Ralph and Colleen will have an even bigger one when they realise they're sharing their home with that great ugly brute.'

'Life is full of surprises.' He kissed her. 'And I doubt they'll care. They'll have other things on their mind — a second chance.'

He lifted their suitcases again.

'Are you coming? Or are you going to stand there looking starry-eyed all day?'

'I'm coming.' Laughing, she stood on tip-toe to kiss him. 'Whither thou goest . . . '

THIS MORTAL COIL

Ann Quinton

'PETS. Exits arranged. Professionally. Effectively. Terminally. Apply: The Coil Shuffler.' Thus reads the business card of a professional assassin. When physiotherapist and lay reader Rachel Morland stumbles across one of these cards on the body of a frail parishioner, her suspicions are at once aroused, not least because she has seen it before — when her beloved husband apparently committed suicide. Policeman Mike Croft, a friend of Rachel's, also realises the significance of the calling-card and, together with his former boss, Nick Holroyd, sets out to track down the killer . . .

GRIANAN

Alexandra Raife

Abandoning her life in England after a broken engagement, Sally flees to Grianan, the beloved Scottish home of her childhood. Running Aunt Janey's remote country house hotel will be a complete break. Sally's brief encounter with Mike — gentle, loving but unavailable — cures the pain of her broken engagement, but leaves a deeper ache in its place. Caught up in the concerns of Grianan, Sally begins to heal. And when fate brings Mike into her life again, tragically altered, she has the strength and faith to hope that Grianan may help him too.

AN INCONSIDERATE DEATH

Betty Rowlands

In the sleepy Gloucestershire village of Marsdean, Lorraine Chant, wife of a wealthy businessman, is found strangled. But why, when both the Chants' safes had been discovered, was nothing stolen? What was Lorraine's relationship with Hugo Bayliss — a man with a dubious background and a penchant for attractive married women? How did Bayliss come to meet Sukey, police photographer and scene of crime officer, before the investigation became public? Then, in a cruel twist of fate, Sukey unwittingly plays into the hands of Lorraine's murderer . . .

THE SIMPLE LIFE

Lauren Wells

Lawrence Langland has had enough of corporate politics and fifteen-hour days. He wants out, to a simpler life. Isobel, his wife, whose gold-plated keyring says 'Born to Shop', has her own reasons for wanting to escape. Fortunately for Jacob, their eight-year-old son, it means leaving his horrible boarding school, although his elder sister Dory needs more persuading. And so the Langlands become 'downshifters', exchanging a comfortable house in suburbia for a small cottage in the countryside. Making the decision was the easy part — but can they cope with the reality?